Love and Life in LUCKNOW

Love and Life in Lucknow

An Imaginary Biography of a City

Mehru Jaffer

olive turtle
NIYOGI BOOKS

Published by
NIYOGI BOOKS
Block D, Building No. 77,
Okhla Industrial Area, Phase-I,
New Delhi-110 020, INDIA
Tel: 91-11-26816301, 26818960
Email: niyogibooks@gmail.com
Website: www.niyogibooksindia.com

Editor: Saachi Khurana
Design: Shraboni Roy

ISBN: 978-93-86906-22-9
Publication: 2018

Printed at: Niyogi Offset Pvt. Ltd., New Delhi, India

For Jaffar and Ali, my sons.
Both master storytellers and
champion listeners.

CONTENTS

Introduction	9
Lakshman Tila	18
Tales of May and June	43
Vision of Claude Martin and Gori Bibi	50
The Anglo-Indians	60
Morning Walk	69
Naresh the Rickshawala	76
Who does Bano Bua Think she is?	83
My Grandmother	89
The Courtesan	95
More Myths	114
Kabir Das	119
Munna Bhai	125
Muharram Then and Now	134
Muharram and a Marriage	148
The Who's Who of Avadh	158
Sahara City	172
Trouble on the Street	176
Shah Najaf	184
Tamboli Begum	189
Acknowledgements	200

INTRODUCTION

Here are some stories from Lucknow, my hometown. This is a city overflowing with stories more luminous than the gems in Aladdin's cave. This is because people who come here bring a bagful of experiences gathered from their wanderings around the globe. Another word for wealth is the confluence of existing folklores, legends, myths and nostalgia with the anticipation of newcomers. The constant supply of new ideas and vocabularies over centuries has enriched the city's cultural treasury, propelling Lucknow to emerge as a wonderful world of contrasts.

Citizens continue to make up stories as they serve as a safeguard against the vagaries of times both terrific and trying. When suspicion grips the city, storytellers step in to imagine ways of transforming all that is life-threatening into something divine, and to coax citizens into feeling like each one of them is part of the same big family. The role of stories is so central to our lives that making them up is a profession preferred by some. Stories are floated by the wicked as well, with the intent to create a rift between human beings, but in the end the majority of citizens choose to love rather than hate each other. It has taken the city aeons to consciously teach itself to celebrate and not to resent other human beings. In this land of abundance the practice is to quarrel less and to enjoy the bounties of nature more. It is the habit of long-time residents and community leaders to appreciate life in all its rainbow-coloured contradictions, inspiring generations after them to do the same. The more imaginative ones have learnt to recount the fate of human existence in enchantingly different ways. Those with a special gift of the gab are a pampered lot. They are encouraged to concoct as many stories as they can about what love and life are, sometimes for the sole purpose of simply dazzling the senses.

Some storytellers groom their thoughts in vocabulary that may sound unreal, impossible and exaggerated at first. But ask the listener and he or she will cross the heart and ask for more, insisting that the stories told here, by God, are to die for. No wonder few like to leave Lucknow, forcing a motley crowd of citizens to practice that generous philosophy called "live and let live". There are many who will tell you how they have emerged from yesterday's visitor to today's host. All sorts of people are attracted to this land since times lost to memory, mainly because there is plenty to eat here. Human beings from far away have crossed seas, scaled mountains, trudged across deserts to make a home in Lucknow.

Of course, many have also battled with each other to get as close as possible to the lush fields laden all year round with a vast variety of fruits, grains and vegetables. But in the end everyone realises how disastrous it is to turn rich farmlands into killing fields. This is one of the most fertile areas of the Indo-Gangetic plains due to rich deposits of clay, silt, and sand brought by the many rivers that flow through the flat plains, with ground water gurgling in plenty. The land is perfect for large-scale farming and, once here, the only ambition is to live happily ever after. This quest for contentment is at the core of all stories, including the ones I bring to you in this book.

Some of the stories shared with you today are those I remember from childhood. They were told to me by elders whose imagination seems to have worked overtime. The number of stories responsible for making my childhood magical are many, but the one that remains topmost in my memory is about Mr and Mrs Mint Leaf. I am unable to forget this amazing couple, as the story had the power to make rivers vanish into their ear, according to my grandmother. The story of Mr and Mrs Mint Leaf is not included in this volume, as I am unable to recall the punchline. But there are other stories I have made up for you. Some are inspired from real-life experiences. The most recent story picked up by me in Lucknow is about Jyoti and Jahan Ara.

At first glance it is easy to mistake the two for sisters. Both women share a similar look. They speak the same dialect of Hindi and enjoy a common sense of humour. But Jyoti and Jahan Ara are not from the same family. They are just close friends. They have also been neighbours in a lower-middle-class township in one of the most congested parts of Lucknow for years.

One day Jyoti realised that Jahan Ara had lost her job as household help in several non-Muslim homes. She was angry.

She wanted to help her poor friend to continue to earn a living. She thought of a plan and introduced Jahan Ara as Bitti to affluent families living in a large, upmarket housing society. In local dialect, *bitti* means "little girl", from the original word *bitia,* used by both Hindu and Muslim families to address a girl child. The name Bitia does not betray one's religion, unlike Jyoti, which is distinctly Hindu, and Jahan Ara, which is Muslim.

Jyoti's little plan has worked. From my balcony I watch them giggling together as they go from apartment to apartment cleaning and swabbing the floor and cooking for some families. It makes me happy to see that all is well with them. I feel upbeat about the fact that friendship between at least two human beings in the city holds far more value than religion.

There are other stories. I tell of times when the sigh of a lover was able to light up lamps in the city. You will come across stories from days when more trees had lined the streets than fake Victorian lamps. Like in most stories, there is a hero in this book as well. The hero is the citizen. The hero is Naresh the *rickshawala*—or would you rather call him *nautankibaaz*? It is the sadhu on the street, the vegetable vendor, the milkman and the newspaper boy. Tell me if you think Bano Bua, the bully, is the lead character in this book, or if it is the temperamental Tamboli Begum. What about lovable Jamila Jan? Can someone who finds mention in one important part of the story be considered a heroine as well? Perhaps that solitary figure manning the last carriage still drawn by a horse in town is heroic, too? You decide.

And if the hero is here and all the leading ladies are here, can the villain be far behind? The villain has to be the one who stands in the way of social harmony. The villain has to be the negative energy that prevents human beings from indulging in great values like love, grace, togetherness, selflessness and humility.

The many characters in the book are assembled from different recesses of the region, from its imaginary past to records preserved in archives and in history books. Portraits have been pulled out from the present in the hope that the varied experiences of others may help us to find a clue or two on how to treat other human beings with more respect in the future.

The stories are inspired by local heroes and villains in Avadh, a corner of the country that has been unique since prehistoric times. I am sure that extraordinary cultures exist in other parts of the world, too, but my world is Avadh. It is this world and the people who live here that I am most familiar with, whose stories I know best and am eager to share with you.

Avadh is the ancient name of the present-day territory of Uttar Pradesh, of which Lucknow is the state capital. Avadh is unique, because different people in different times and in their own way have been trying for centuries to teach themselves to deal with other human beings a little more gently.

Avadh is just another way of pronouncing Ayodhya by people of Persian origin, who came here as warriors and economic migrants. Ayodhya was once the imperial capital of Rama, the god-king. Rama was so beloved of the people he ruled that, over time, he was elevated to one of the many reincarnations of Vishnu. Before Ayodhya, the city was called Saket, which means "paradise", and it is here that the Buddha had meditated most intensely.

Gautam Buddha was born 2,600 years ago, further east of Lucknow in Lumbini in modern-day Nepal. But at the ancient site of Saket he had paused to preach 600 years before the birth of Jesus Christ. His many followers practiced Buddhism for about a thousand years, after which people in Avadh chose to experience life from a different perspective, once they were introduced to other ideas they found equally exciting. People from Central Asia were familiar with Avadh long before Islam marched into this land with more warriors of Turkic origin in the 11th century. The followers of Islam in India have been impressed by Hinduism but they have resisted converting to the dominant religion. They choose to remain both Indian and Muslim at the same time. Besides, Hinduism has a flair for absorbing, and not necessarily battling, every new idea and identity that crosses its path.

Even as they continue to practice Islam, Muslims find Hinduism attractive enough to have given birth to the Ganga-Jamuni way of life. Like the confluence of the rivers Ganga and Yamuna, Hinduism and Islam have come together in such a way that the interest of one does not adversely affect the other in Avadh. Such is the soil of Avadh. Such is the air and water of the place that those who are fortunate to touch upon this land blossom into creatures unlike others in the world.

Even the yogi is different. Most of the time he enjoys a more poetic sync with the solar system. He shines brighter than Sirius in the sky and believes that love is a good reason to be alive. He points to the importance of colours because different tones rescue life from the monotony of black and white. Rama and Krishna are often painted in blue to suggest the inclusive nature of both, but the yogi is draped in saffron to signal maturity and new beginnings.

In the past many yogis have led lives of great responsibility in Avadh. Will *this* yogi at the helm of affairs in Uttar Pradesh today be as caring as some of his spiritual ancestors? Or will he soil the age-old reputation of the best yogis of Avadh, who have made great efforts in the past to help communities to battle confusion and cruelty, and to overcome fear and insecurity?

Yogis have contributed considerably to the flowering of a variety of local ideas of worship. The landscape is dotted with numerous places of worship for different deities that guard every village. Into this pantheon of existing gods and goddesses, Muslim mystics and their reverence for the shrines of their spiritual masters found an easy niche. It is not unusual for a Hindu to meditate at the tomb of a Muslim mystic or for a Muslim poet to appreciate the love of Radha for Krishna. What Muslim mystics and Hindu mendicants have in common is a lifelong search for that wondrous energy responsible for the birth of everything. It is a personal journey for both to seek out more about whatever is more beautiful and more powerful than they are in life.

Mystic Islam has always been open to local influences, but it continues to follow its own path without getting lost in any one of the many ideas that surround it in Avadh. Local communities are organised in a hierarchical caste system that is unfair to those at the lowest end of the social ladder. When Islam talks of social justice, universal brotherhood and equality among all human beings, the outcasts, who are also the majority population, sit up and listen. The egalitarian ideals of Islam tempt the unwanted in society. In the early 12th century, when Muslims decided that they were here to stay, devout Hindus made their worship more public. Local deities like Rama and Krishna were shared with the masses. The 16th-century poet Goswami Tulsidas translated the *Ramayana* into the local dialect of Avadhi, spoken in the countryside. This later text spread the idea of a perfect Rama among the large majority of ordinary citizens who did not have access to the story of Rama as told earlier (originally in Sanskrit) by Valmiki. The annual fair held in honour of Rama in 19th-century Ayodhya is remembered as an impressive event that attracted thousands of pilgrims.

That people from different corners of the globe have been visiting Avadh for thousands of years is not surprising. The landscape of Avadh is attractive to behold and to live in. It is part of the great alluvial plain of the Ganga. As mentioned earlier, the flat and fertile land with narrow fields grows lots of food. The long and winding rivers nourish a series of crops cultivated here and are responsible for lush greenery all around.

The beauty of the landscape and distinct seasons have transformed many a warrior into a poet. Although modern-day lyricist Shailendra was no sword-wielding warrior, he was soaked in the poetic traditions of the nearby city of Mathura. This is the area where Lord Krishna was born and spent his childhood romancing Radha, the love of his life. Shailendra had carried much of the romance of Mathura with him when he moved to Mumbai in the late 1940s. He wrote poetry that impressed film makers. Soon his love songs became part of many Bollywood films, including this song, which is translated by me from the original Hindi:

> Come home, my love,
> The dark clouds are dangerously near.

> The heartbeat quickens at the sound of thunder,
> And lightning fills me with fear.
> The silence of loneliness haunts.
> My love, come home,
> I wait by the window
> Drenched in the monsoon of want,
> And thirsting...

From July to January the rivers are full and the trees are laden with fruits. Avadh dries up during the summer months of April and June, when the region is carpeted in deathlike silence till a dust storm arrives to wake people up and to remind them that there is much to look forward to after the storm has blown over. And true to the words of nature, when the monsoons follow in July, the grey of the heat is washed away and all living creatures are persuaded to rejoice and to revel once more in the myriad colours of life.

What is common in all the stories told today is our continuing curiosity over mysteries like: what is life? What is love? Till we find answers to similar questions that keep human beings mystified, storytellers will continue to imagine, in even more tales to come, all those aspects of life that remain so elusive, so intangible.

All translations, unless otherwise specified, are by me.

LAKSHMAN TILA

I wait for the caravan of stars to light my way before stepping out of the house to climb the Lakshman Tila. To match the moonlight, I drape myself in two and a half yards of fine, cream-coloured chiffon. I like to look good when I go to the Lakshman Tila.

I head for that corner on the *tila* where all the four elements of air, earth, fire and water are in such supreme harmony that, if there is a secret of existence, I feel it is sure to be experienced here. I look at the chiffon I carry with me that is scattered in knots made by the city's female embroiderers using a needle and several strands of silver thread. The chiffon makes me feel as if all the heavenly bodies of the galaxy have fallen into my lap.

The Lakshman Tila is Lucknow's highest mound, but it is low enough to reach as often as desire dictates. The heavens feel close up here although the feet remain grounded. Reason may inspire the climb to the *tila*, but it is possible to find romance here. It is said that, once, a single seed of a wish was enough to sprout a variety of vegetation on the *tila* and in its vicinity. That is before the alluvial soil was plastered with so much concrete.

A few trees both tall and short still stand on the elevated earth that is crumbling down towards the roads below. Patches of grass cling to a rapidly balding landscape, but the few birds that still come to nest here remember to bring their songs with them. It is true that fewer animals roam the *tila* now, and many of its residents spend most of their time protecting relics left from the past by ancestors who have both inspired and repulsed humanity. Bano Bua likes to come to the *tila* because it is the home of the Baba of the Bottles. I like to come to the *tila* because it is one place in the city that makes me feel high. Any time feels just right to be on top of the *tila.* For it is always less warm here but never cool enough to make one shiver.

The Gomti, a tributary of the Ganga, runs past the base of the *tila,* mirroring stories collected over timelessness, during its endless meanderings.

Who is Bano Bua, you may ask? Let's just say that my Bano Bua is the most bewitching *dastango,* or storyteller, in the world. She spins stories more baffling than a spider's web.

This is not surprising, as once upon a time the city was home to a crowd of storytellers who elevated the Urdu language to new heights. Urdu was born nearly a thousand years ago in the army barracks of Turkic warriors who chose Delhi as their seat of power in 1192. The mostly Farsi-speaking Turkic soldiers must have pulled out a smattering of vocabulary borrowed from Farsi, Turkic and local dialects to string together odd sentences in an effort to communicate with each other. The Turkic word for the army to this day is Ordusu, and Ordu is a port city on the

Black Sea coast in modern-day Turkey, so called because while it was still a village it was upgraded in medieval times to an army outpost.

As the warriors of Turkic and Persian origin moved further into the heartland of the Indian subcontinent, the language was nourished on a diet of local soil and air. Eventually a strong tradition of speech took root here, which poets compare to a pearl from the sea of eloquence and a dazzling noon of rhetoric.

Luckily the conquerors did not confine Urdu to the four walls of the court but shared the language with the entire city. That is why poetically inspired thoughts, similes and metaphors come naturally even to ordinary citizens of this city. A very good example of the unique way that the people of Lucknow live and use language is the glittering art of *dastangoi,* or extempore storytelling.

Around the 19th century, a form of orally recited romance in prose came into being. This passionate interest in human relationships was elaborated on and transmitted by professional raconteurs, who told stories in Urdu that became immensely popular because of their universal appeal.

The art of *dastangoi* was already popular in the royal courts of neighbouring Persia and most of the stories were mainly inspired by ancient folk tales. When Farsi-speaking people came to India, their stories came with them. As rulers of this part of north India, they encouraged the art of creating stories to explore the enigmatic roles of love, hate and loss in life. That is how raconteurs multiplied to enthrall private audiences, patrons, and the public at large. Among numerous narratives, *The Adventures of Amir Hamza,* originally told in Farsi, became popular in Urdu.

Over time, many Indian tales were added to Hamza's Persian adventures and recited in late 18th-century Mughal India, often in the beauteous gardens of that time.

In 1858, Munshi Naval Kishore founded the famous Lucknow press. Apart from textbooks and literary works, he also published the stories of Hamza's adventures in Urdu between 1893 and 1908. This was the first time that these stories recited orally were preserved forever in print. Compiled by Muhammad Husain Jah and Ahmad Husain Qamar, *Tilism Hoshruba* or "The Land of Enchantment" is one of the legends from the many adventures of Hamza, full of wondrous prose and poetry.

The *dastango* has always been free to dive into the well of words before surfacing with over a billion interpretations and possibilities of the way life can be lived on this planet. Lest listeners come out of the dazzle, the stories are told in a poetically musical way, creating a world of utter wonder where words slay easier than a sword, and audiences are left to imagine shadows of giants on large screens of fog and mist created with words. In the world of a *dastango*, there are fishes that have their mouths full of pearls, and handsome mares that whisper sweet nothings into the ears of the human beings they love.

Even before the adventures of Hamza made it to Lucknow, folk narratives were recited routinely in the city. Stories about everyday life were shared and circulated orally in some form or the other. Prose had always existed here and romantic fairy tales and heroic legends were seldom lacking in popular imagination. Over time the existing folk legends about demons, god-men, and half-human, half-animal creatures intertwined into all the narrations from Persia till the stories were neither Hindu nor Muslim. The stories became a favourite of everyone who enjoyed having their imagination tickled, and were interested in everything that exists beyond the world of humans.

By the 19th century, telling stories and religiously listening to lore became one of the most popular pastimes in the city, when one *dastango* better than the other took to the stage dressed in loose robes of fine white muslin that were embroidered in thread even whiter. The button had just been introduced to India from Europe. In Lucknow, a waistcoat up to the neck became a fashion, with buttons running down in the front and worn above see-through frock-like garments fashioned in many a frivolous cut. The *dastango* may have also worn a matching skullcap and squatted on expensive carpets spread out on the floor under the canopy of a midnight-blue sky, lit up by stars. Huddled in a circle of shadows thrown up by their own flickering soul, the *dastango* must have delighted in leading his bewitched audiences to wherever his wild imagination had wished to travel.

The tales continued in winter time. The air was thick then, with fires lit in sandalwood, the smoke of which mingled with rose blossoms rambling all over the city as if in search of an even more rare lore of life. In high summer it was the aroma of the jasmine blossoms that kept the city intoxicated and helped audiences to fuel their fantasy to keep pace with that of the storyteller.

The *dastango* was inspired by musical renditions of the local *kathakar*. These were nomadic storytellers who entertained a different audience each night in a different part of the region, with *katha* or tales often dramatised with song and dance, mainly in praise of the deep love between Krishna and Radha.

When the supremely entertaining *kathak* attracted the attention of the king, he was invited to settle down at the court to regale royalty.

Eventually storytelling, dance and music combined to give birth to Kathak, a classical dance form that is popular to this day. Today Bano Bua may be a lone *dastango* in a city, but she is the best. Bua is a word that Hindus use for an aunt who is a sister of the father. But for ages Muslim families have endearingly called their household help Bua. Although I suspect that my Bano Bua is a cross between a waif and a witch, really, and she means much more to me today than a mere maidservant.

It is Bano Bua who tells me that the *tila* was the love of Lakshman of the *Ramayana*. It has served as a safe haven for soldiers and a home for hermits, and once was the main marketplace of the masses. For sure the story of Lucknow begins at the Lakshman Tila. It is Rama who chose this hillock in Lucknow on the southern side of the laid-back Gomti as a home for his beloved brother, Lakshman. Rama must have taken this decision on a day when the heavens were without cloud and the light from the full moon had made night seem bright. With the breeze fanning him, the aroma of the jasmine blossom must have longed to mingle with his sweat out of love for Rama while birds serenaded his sauntering in the woods. Then Rama must have decided to gift the *tila* to Lakshman. He must have also tried to attract Sita's attention by pelting her with a petunia to make sure that he got a nod of approval from her. Sita at that moment must have swayed on a lotus-shaped rock and found it difficult to look away from across the river, where a row of thirsty deer drank to their heart's content.

Later Lakshman spent his days on the same *tila*, carpeted at that time with many more flowers and trees laden with fruits. Lakshman lived in the company of local people, only 300 kilometres west to the kingdom of Ayodhya, where Rama, the seventh incarnation of Lord Vishnu, was now king. If Rama is Vishnu, then the devoted Lakshman is revered as an incarnation of the cobra, who curled into a cosmos couch so that his good brother could rest his eyes in-between the task of keeping order in the world. Rama is worshipped to this day for his magnanimity of having shared His Majesty with all his subjects, including the local potter, the weaver, the sweeper and the boatman. Because of their love for Rama and Lakshman, the *tila* became the abode of ardent devotees of the cobra, the king of snakes.

The other legend about the origins of the Lakshman Tila goes back to times when aspersions were cast on the fidelity of a pregnant Sita. Rama had requested Lakshman to escort Sita away from the palace and the unstoppable gossip in Ayodhya to the peace and quiet of the hut of Valmiki in the forests nearby. Since nobody knows the truth, the storyteller is believed when it is said that on the way from Ayodhya, Lakshman and Sita broke their journey in Lucknow on this *tila*, which was later named after Lakshman. The magic of the lofty, languid landscape continued to attract people from different corners of the world, like the Chinese, Greeks, Slavs and members of nomadic tribes of Central Asia, much after Lakshman and Sita left, tempting thieves to steal from there and others to further enrich the environs with new ideas in farming and in architecture. The meadow is said by a local storyteller to be more delightful than the Garden of Eden, its flowers shining like jewels on the green expanse.

In the same garden the girls are described in *Hoshruba* as coquettish and as stately as the sun in the heavens. They are between the ages of 15 and 16 years, familiar with the pangs of adolescence, and with nights of desire. Among them is a princess whose beauty is the envy of the moon.

Centuries later, when beliefs passed down from the past stopped making sense in the present, people must have looked for new ideas to inspire them. When the image of Rama became too distant and remote, devotion to a much more playful Krishna as the next incarnation of Vishnu must have emerged.

Tales about Krishna's defeat of Kaliya—a cobra crowned with multiple menacing heads, filled with poison and polluting the neighbouring waters of the river Yamuna—were circulated, and images of Krishna in the company of cows became popular. Clearly it was time to replace cobra worship with cow worship. Numerous other stories of Krishna's valour spread across the entire expanse of the verdant lands of the shisham, *peepal*, neem, and mango thickets. Listening to the many stories of bravado, and charmed by the music made by Krishna on the flute as he grazed cattle in the verdant forests of Vrindavan, crowds in this part of the world were transported into a trance. Those supremely awestruck danced with joy at being in love all over again. This way the mercurial affection of human beings shifted from Laxman and the cobra to Krishna and the cow, and the previous power and influence of the community of snake worshippers at the Lakshman Tila diminished.

Despite countless adoring him, the child consciousness of Krishna remains self-conscious. This is what makes Krishna lovable; he possesses all the cleverness of a god and yet mortals identify with his complaints, which are similar to their own. It is difficult for Krishna to come to terms with the contradiction that he is born high but forced to share the colour of his skin with those considered the lowest in society.

Krishna's greatest complex over his swarthy complexion continues to tickle the imagination of painters and poets, who try to tackle the child god's angst by juggling words into different combinations. Here is a popular folk song that is translated from the original Hindi by me:

> Why are both,
> Brother Balaram and beloved Radha,
> So light?
> Why am I not also as white?

Before the arrival of Rama and Krishna, the Lakshman Tila was a terrace of the sacred Brahma Desa landscape. The land was eventually fortified by nomadic tribes who had strayed into the plains from mountains further north, many millennia ago. The comfort provided by the pristine pastures made them stay on. The land was bursting in plenty with all that is deliciously edible, and there was plenty of time left for thought. Concepts like creation and cosmology was a concern. A large part of the day was spent staring at the sun and at night it was realised how beautiful the moon is.

The residents of the Lakshman Tila and of around the area must have found the deep meditations of the visitors harmless, and even mindless. Who knows? It might have amused them to listen to wistful hymns composed in praise of the beauteous land, whose abundance the locals may have taken for granted.

After years of philosophising over matters relating to life and death, a certain view of the world came to take root here:

that the Brahmin is born from Brahma, the only reality in an endless existence of illusion. It was whispered that the Brahmin alone is chosen to receive the Vedic words of eternal wisdom that had dropped verse by verse into Brahma's lotus-shaped lap during each meditation. Tales of the prowess of the privileged Brahmin were so convincing that the rest of the population was silenced into belief. Besides, the majority of the population had little time left from fulfilling mundane chores of buying, selling, sowing, harvesting and cleaning to challenge any philosophy.

Only the warrior, appointed second in the social hierarchy to the Brahmin, was permitted an occasional glimpse into the secrets of the sanctum sanctorum built inside the ivory towers owned by a privileged few. The descendants of the rest of society were gradually pushed to the periphery of their own land. They resented the fact that they were distanced from the sacred sphere of life. All spiritual activity was dominated by a minority group of people who made themselves comfortable on the crown of the social ladder. It took several centuries before solace came with the birth of the Buddha, who said that, spiritually speaking, every part of the human being is sacred, including the feet, from where the majority of local people were told they had originated.

Born high in the social skyscraper, the Buddha chose to spend a lifetime in the basement of life, with the masses who struggled to come to terms with injustices on their own. The Buddha inspired even the most humble in the flock to stop pining for the high priest and to seek the creator on his or her own.

Many of the Buddha's compassionate conclusions about life were drawn during his meditations in different parts of Avadh, and his followers like to trek in the footsteps of the wise one.

In the 5th century, Fahsien, the Chinese Buddhist, passed through Lucknow on his way to Ayodhya and looked forward to meeting other Buddhist monks who lived there. The desire of all pilgrims is similar. It is to breathe the same air as the Buddha had in Avadh. This land was part of ancient Saket, where the enlightened one had taught for over two decades. Huien Tsang, another Chinese monk, spent time at Hulas Kheda in Lucknow during his travels in the 7th century. Some Buddhist temples remain in Lucknow, although the number of devotees is modest compared to the crowds seen at other places of worship.

All places of worship are considered sacred by most people in Lucknow. It is warriors and conquerors who demolish works of art and architecture, not ordinary citizens. A crescent moon and a star crowns the pinnacle of one temple donated probably by a Muslim devotee. Devotees enjoy the freedom to visit any place of worship they wish to in the city. According to architect Vipul B. Varshney, Lucknow is the land of ancient people called Pratiharas, Nagas and Rajputs, who built numerous temples for the goddess Durga.

The Sheetla Devi temple is one of the oldest. It has its origins in the *Ramayana* era and was built by Lava, son of Rama. The Muslim rulers of Lucknow took care of this temple. Another favourite of both Hindu and Muslim devotees is the Chanchi Kuan Hanuman temple. The temple displays different architectural styles because the original structure has been renovated through donations by different people at different times in history. What was a Hindu place of worship sometimes became a place of pilgrimage for Buddhists and later a sanctuary for Jains. Today, prayers are chanted by any devotee on the premises of the Kalyangiri complex of originally Jain temples, similar to those on Gujrat's Girnar hills. The temple complex includes a place of worship for Shiva, Ram, Lakshman, Janki and Santoshi Mata.

The sage and the sorcerer both came here. Swordsmen came to conquer the place, but many a wanderer also succumbed to the serenity of the surroundings to be transformed into a sage. It is on the Lakshman Tila that many meditated to find out what is sinful in life and what is not.

Shah Mina was born in the vicinity in the 14th century and he impressed the local people with his simple living and his generosity towards all human beings.

Having made a little luggage of all the kindness that he had experienced in life, the sage spent his days matching the Islam of the book to daily practices, like love and generosity. His doors were forever open to every visitor and he attended to anyone in hunger, pain or suffering. For the same reason, his abode was always crowded with devotees and the neighbourhood he lived in became famous as Mina Nagri.

Shah Mina followed in the tradition of mystics like Muinuddin Chishti, who came to India in 1191 from Persian lands. Chishti was made to feel at home in the desert town of Ajmer in Rajasthan simply because the local people were overjoyed by his presence in their midst. He continues to be revered today as Garib Nawaz, "friend of the poor". Shah Mina believed in one creator of the world. He practiced universal brotherhood, peace and equality among all humankind. He befriended every creature that crossed his path. Shah Mina was loved for the ease with which he could see an entire world in the eyes of a human being. People flocked around the sage because he could show them joy in the heart of a flower. In his presence crowds woke up to the joy of being alive. Those who went to him became aware of the significance of each thud of the heart. People rarely returned home without feeling that life is only about loving other human beings. The people around him saw how Shah Mina respected all human beings irrespective of the way they looked and of preferences for a different language, dress or food.

Shah Mina died in Lucknow in 1465, leaving behind a legacy of ideas similar to the expressions of love already popular in verses from the *Gita Govinda.* These are songs of Krishna, composed by Jayadeva, a 12th-century bhakti poet devoted to the love between Radha and Krishna: "Because of your separation from her, the home of Radha is turned into wilderness..."

The 15th-century poet, Kabir, speaks of similar love for his beloved:

> Bring your face nearer to his ear,
> And speak of deep longings of the heart.
> Says Kabir, Listen to me, oh brother!
> Picture with the eyes,
> In the heart vision of the beloved other.

While the prince rules by precept, poets make people surrender to the words they wield. The most popular poets are those who speak in the language of the majority of people. Poets realise that verse is manna for the masses, who know not how to read or to write, but can hear everything. Recitations in the people's language help to un-puzzle the world for ordinary citizens. Most mystics are therefore poets or love poetry.

Among Muslim mystics, the practice is to bury the sage where he lived and meditated. It is an old tradition for devotees from far and near to pilgrimage to the earthly domain of a beloved human being who is no more, in the hope of experiencing some of the goodness spread by the good soul. Talk to people living on the Lakshman Tila and listen to them say that a visit to the place where the pious perish increases one's spiritual focus. The shrine of a sage is one place where all of humanity is able to unburden itself of social loads like "low-born" and "high-born".

The tomb of Shah Mina is a fine example of the celebration of togetherness among human beings. The crowds peak during *urs,* the death anniversary of a sage, which in mystical terms implies spiritual awakening. With the end of life on Earth, a soul is said to dissolve back into the supreme consciousness from where life originates. While birth separates, in death the soul flows back like a stray stream into the eternal ocean of consciousness. The idea that death makes existence whole once again fills pilgrims at the *urs* of a sage with ecstasy.

The Lakshman Tila attracted Shah Pir Muhammad—another sage from the Chishti school of mysticism—who died here in 1673. He is remembered as a great teacher who was accepting of the many definitions of truth. He taught himself to find beauty in all the different and often competing views of the world. What preoccupied him most was sheer wonder at existence and a love for all life. He is buried on the Lakshman Tila under a square-shaped mausoleum topped with a dome, near a mosque later built perhaps by Sultan Ali, governor of Avadh during the reign of Aurangzeb.

The mausoleum of both Shah Mina and Shah Pir Muhammad are full of life. The premises throb with a swarm of devotees still in love with people, so long after they are no more. To the pilgrim the physical presence is less important than the great ideas gifted to humanity by good human beings. Several seekers therefore continue to stream around the shrine of a sage irrespective of walls that try to box human beings into a corner and to divide them in the name of caste, class, gender and religion.

THE BABA OF THE BOTTLES

To get to the Baba of the Bottles, Bano Bua must first conquer the Tila from one end, and then slide down a pitch-dark entrance on the opposite side before entering a cave in the bowel of the Tila. She always carries a bag, inside of which is a bottle. After making sure that the bottle is no longer moist from washing, she rolls a note of money and neatly slides it into the bottle.

Every time she is restless, confused or suffers insecurity, Bano Bua performs this exercise and hastens to see the Baba of the Bottles. If for some reason it is not possible for her to have an audience with the Baba of the Bottles, she makes a little bundle of rose petals, incense sticks and candles, and gets Naresh to pull her on his rickshaw all the way to Nadan Mahal Road, a crowded area near the old city of Lucknow. This is a neighbourhood from the 16th century. Apart from homes and numerous shops, there are several tombs in a nearby park. The first tomb Bano Bua visits bears the mortal remains of Ibrahim Chishti, a mystic who lived in Lucknow in the 16th century. Devotees come here in the hope of *nidan* or moksha or liberation. The neighbourhood of Nadan Mahal gets its name from *nidan*.

Bano Bua makes sure that her head is covered as she moves to the marble memorial of Sheikh Abdur Rahim in the same park. Here she once again offers prayers and lights several incense sticks and candles, before closing her eyes in a few minutes of meditation. The caretakers at the premises will tell you that the Sheikh was dear to Emperor Akbar and became more so after a curious incident. Astrologers had once warned Emperor Akbar that he should beware two days when bad luck could visit him, and Akbar decided to give up the throne for those two days.

However, Akbar did not want the affairs of the empire to be disrupted during that time. He asked his advisors what he should do. A senior official at court, the Sheikh was the first to volunteer to sit on the throne instead of Akbar for the inauspicious period. Akbar agreed and all went well till a eunuch responsible for the royal laundry suddenly passed away. He had died of a snakebite from a cobra that was found slithering in the pile of clothes meant for Akbar.

Ever since, Akbar felt that he owed his life to the Sheikh. Akbar was grateful to the Sheikh and gifted him land in Lucknow. The Sheikh came there to overpower rebellious local feudal lords. On the Lakshman Tila he built a grand residence for himself and called it the Machchi Bhawan, because it was decorated with glistening figures of 52 fishes. Close by, he also built the Panch Mahal or "Five Palaces" for his children.

When the Sheikh died he was buried at Nadan Mahal, and his Brahmin wife Krishna beautified the surroundings of the tomb with a garden. The premises were always open to the public. Krishna made sure that weary souls were welcomed in this paradise on Earth and that the hungry always found food here. In memory of the Sheikh and of Krishna, Bano Bua always leaves a little money for those taking care of the premises before returning to the rickshaw of the waiting Naresh.

At the abode of the Baba of the Bottles, Bano Bua surrenders both the bottle and herself to the enlightened one, who enjoys the reputation of knowing everything without being told anything. There are rumours that the Baba of the Bottles is not a god, man, animal, stone or plant, and that he was never born—nor will he ever die. He is there and yet is never there. Above all he is able to converse with the cobra, the *khalifa* and the Catholic alike and often at the same time.

In the sanctuary of her beloved Baba of the Bottles, Bano Bua sits in utter patience and in total silence for her turn to be addressed. It does not distract her that the Baba sits before a mountain of bottles of every shape, size and colour to gaze at whatever he wants and for as long as he likes. And that his legs are so lost somewhere beneath his torso that they seem not to exist.

The Baba of the Bottles takes the bottle from each visitor and tugs the paper money out of it. He irons out the note with the palm of his hand and while he does so, the money magically turns into a clean chit of paper, on which he scribbles a prescription. With arms that stretch longer than his body he gives the prescription to the one looking for a cure. But the Baba keeps the bottle, adding to his collection of endless others.

This time Bano Bua wants the Baba of the Bottles to see me because she is worried that I may never get married. The seriously comic Bano Bua, with a slight figure and a heart as big as a boulder but not nearly as hard, says that she is no longer able to look into my eyes. This is because she thinks she has failed to fulfil her duty of organising a wedding for me. Bano Bua finds it extremely unfair that I am single. Who will take care of me after she is gone, is the worry of Bano Bua.

When I say that I can take care of myself, Bano Bua protests. When I say that I am 50 years old, Bano Bua looks at me as if I am still a baby. When I say that nature is so unpredictable that I could die before her, she is beside herself with sorrow and anger. She wants me to stop talking rubbish. She wants the Baba of the Bottles to help me to stop talking rubbish.

I tell her that I have a generous salary from Lucknow University. I have written my first screenplay for a full-length feature film that will be released soon. I am in love with my job, my books, my friends, my life, but none of this abundance that I enjoy is good enough for Bano Bua. According to her, life is most about having a husband. That she herself has never enjoyed a husband is another story, to be told another time.

At this moment Bano Bua believes that I need to be "cured" immediately of my spinsterhood. Since her Baba is the remedy of all ills, she insists on taking me to him. I don't have an iota of faith in any baba, but I agree to go for an audience with the Baba of the Bottles to make Bano Bua happy.

The news from the Baba of the Bottles is that he will see us after dusk.

I feel happy following Bano Bua to the Baba of the Bottles because I love a visit to the Lakshman Tila, any time. I bow low in respect before him before sitting down beside Bano Bua. We wait for our turn to be noticed. I spy one devotee shedding silent tears in a corner, and another curled up against the opposite wall in deep sleep. On my left is a woman rocking a baby in her arms, and a child draws patterns on the mud floor. There is absolute calm in the cave.

When my turn comes, I look up and imagine that the presence of the Baba of the Bottles resembles a question mark. He raises an eyebrow in anticipation of my answer. He wants to know if not being married is a problem with me. When Bano Bua wants to intervene, she is told not to by the Baba of the Bottles.

Bano Bua is forced to listen for a change as the Baba of the Bottles wants me to speak up.

I tell the Baba of the Bottles that it bothers me to be surrounded by people who respect marriage more than love. I tell him about Rehana, who vanished from our lives while we were still in our teens. Rehana was a woman who seemed so fond of Usha that everyone wondered what was going on between the two of them. Usha came from a well-known business family in the city that was affluent and influential. Perhaps Usha's family, especially her father and brothers, warned and threatened the two girls to stop seeing each other. The girls defied the bullying and refused to part company. It can only be suspected that Rehana was kidnapped and surely killed,because she disappeared from the city one day. Her relatives, who continue to mourn their loss, did what they could to trace her whereabouts, but they never saw Rehana ever again.

The memory of Rehana still haunts me. It makes me wonder what human relationships are about. Will there ever be a moment when a human being will stand up for a fellow human being without caring about the religious, gender, caste and class identity of the other?

I tell the Baba of the Bottles that I don't feel the need to marry till I feel I love the person. Bano Bua wants me to marry so that I can have a home of my own, enjoy a cook, driver and gardener. I remind Bano Bua that I already have all these facilities. I do own the home I live in. I love my job of teaching at the English Literature department of Lucknow University. What I do not have in life is a lover, and if Bano Bua can help the beloved in me find one, of course I will marry.

I did experience romantic love a long time ago in a *Garam Hawa* kind of way. Ali had lived in the house next door. Unlike the present-day borders cast in stone between India and Pakistan, our respective gardens were separated then by little more than a porous wall made of the multi-branched henna bush. The only ammunition along this natural barrier between our homes were the many thorns along each stem of the hedge. We went to school together and were best friends till we also fell in love. We were both 17 years old when Ali's family decided to move to Pakistan.

His parents left. Then his sisters and his brothers. But Ali did not. He continued to live in Lucknow with an aunt. We studied at Lucknow University and the plan was to get married after we graduated. Our examination results were announced one wet and blustery day in July. That day the city was caught in the midst of a blinding dust storm, followed by a thunderstorm. The air was rent with the sound of lightning, and torrential rains poured down upon us for hours. The city was finally cleansed of two months of heat and dust. The monsoons had arrived and Lucknow was cool once again.

We celebrated our academic success at the stall of Shukla *chatwala* in Lalbagh, gulping down pani puri after pani puri to see who ate how many more than the other.

Then a telegram arrived from Karachi to say that Ali's mother had suffered a heart attack. She was in hospital. Naturally Ali dropped everything in Lucknow and rushed to Karachi to visit her. That was alright. What did not seem alright for a long time to me was the fact that he never came back. Worse still, Ali never bothered to tell me that he was never coming back.

I did waste some time waiting for this love to return, and for a while it had seemed like it was the end of the world for me. That it was the end of all love and longing in my life.

But today I look back on the incident and feel that it was just as well. I may have missed out on marriage but I did experience love. Perhaps I still love Ali. I am also happy to have discovered over time that love visits life in so many different and splendid ways. Not just in one man called Ali. Along with that love for Ali, I have been overwhelmed time and time again by love found in the rising sun. It is possible to experience love for the orange oozing out of a sunset, during a boat ride on the Gomti, in the verses of Majaz, in the *purwaia*, the breeze that comes to cool and to caress from the east.

I am in love with Avadhi, with the scent of the parched earth that receives the first drop of rain, with thumri, *dadra* and Kathak, with the nautanki performances of Naresh, and above all with the home where I was born, several generations after the ancestor built it.

I wander to different parts of the world out of curiosity, but I am no muhajir still in search of refuge under the sun. I am fortunate to be able to return to where I feel I belong, and to look forward to resting in peace eternally draped in earth, water and air that I am so familiar, and so much in love with.

For the likes of me, who have faced the challenge of living together with such a variety of human beings for millennia, the thought of spending the rest of my life only with Muslim people is not at all attractive. Those relatives who think otherwise visit me when they can from Pakistan. Many of them are curious about my life in the midst of non-Muslim people. Some come to match the Lucknow in their heads with the way the city really is. There are complaints over how shabby the ancestral home looks under my care. Several of them speak as if they still own and have a right over a way of life they abandoned a long time ago. As if I am somehow responsible for the life across the border that has not worked out for them, for their refugee status and disappointment in a nation of the *pure* that remains wickedly as complex and as colourful as Avadh. As if they come in search of reasons that made their elders leave Lucknow, and, unable to find much, remain irritated throughout their visit to my place.

"What happened to Dadajan's black Buick? Where is that tree, and that bush? You had them chopped? Why? Why did you change the gate and plaster that window my Abbajan had loved so much? Why did you knock that arch away? And the kitchen is now this side...How can you be happy living here? Come to Karachi; I will get you married to a nice Muslim man living in Canada," are taunts of Pakistani relatives I do not want to hear.

One relative could not believe that a city that looks so elegant in photographs framed and exhibited in his home in Karachi is such a dump in reality. The Gomti is time and again declared a stinking drain, and the royal Bengal tigers in the zoo shrink in the eyes of many a cousin from across the border into creatures no bigger than cats.

The worst visitors from Pakistan are those who insist, in a Punjabi accent, that Urdu is dead in Lucknow. They are oblivious of a place called Adabistan in the city, a piece of writing called *Taus Chaman ki Maina,* and of the precious existence of Naiyer Masud, a poet's storyteller.

What is it with the number seven, I want to know from the Baba. In 1857, Muslims together with other Indians were humiliated by colonialists. In 1937 the Indian Congress Party and the Muslim League failed to organise the sharing of political power between them, which made Muslims sulk for decades due to insecurity. That was followed by the partition of India in 1947, and now in 2017 Muslims in Avadh are again at sea over their future.

After the Baba has listened to everything that I have said, the clean chit of paper in his hands turns back into money. The Baba of the Bottles returns the note to me, ignoring Bano Bua's outstretched hand. On the prescription that he gives to Bano Bua, he has scrawled "Tulip Blossom".

"This is the name of someone in Lucknow. That person is the only one in the world who can cure you of your problem, Bano Bua. Your problem, which is as tiny as the tip of a needle, but as annoying as all those forever asking for freedom.

"And once you find out who Tulip Blossom is, go for an audience," suggests the Baba of the Bottles.

Then he hurries us home with the warning that nothing should delay Bano Bua in doing what she must do. The Baba of the Bottles insists that she sweats it out, if she must, but waste no more time, especially in wait for the amorous but totally unreliable monsoons. Bano Bua is asked to comb every corner, sieve every street in the city to find Tulip Blossom. Even in the discomfort of extreme sunshine and without the solace of rain.

"What has to be done must be done. And done now!" the Baba of the Bottles repeats, his arms making lasso-like circles above a head studded with a pair of eyes so wide open that it is possible to peep into the wells of his wisdom.

Bano Bua is happy with the visit. She is in fact happiest when she is busy. Her newly found responsibility fills her with a renewed sense of importance. She plunges into the task of decoding the message of the Baba of the Bottles. And being the kind of person that she is, Bano Bua threatens to turn day into night and night into day, to find out who Tulip Blossom is and how she can help Bano Bua to find a groom for me even at the age of 50 years.

The thought makes me burst into a verse of my own: "For I doubt that crazy will ever be found, to humour the likes of me all the year round..."

TALES OF MAY AND JUNE

This is the time of the year when, due to extreme heat, nothing stirs in Lucknow before sundown. During the day the city is lost in slumber or preoccupied in special prayer. Silent chants spiral skywards from the bottom of the city's heart to get the sun to disappear from life for a while. The entire flatlands at the foot of the Himalayan mountain range play host during peak summer months to such heartless heat that even the air becomes breathless.

Water buffaloes darker than moonless nights dot any water to be found on the flat plains. The earth at this time of the year is reduced to burnt brown wastelands.

Animals squat motionless in shallow swamps evaporated of all slosh. Some deep green foliage left over from springtime is still there, sprayed in sheets of fine dust kicked up by the *loo*—the hot and dry westerly wind that gives the landscape a lifeless look. This is the season when those leaves lucky enough to survive the constant huffing and puffing of the *loo* refuse to sway to a lighter breeze after sunset in fear of falling off the branches. And nightingales are left with beaks open, bewildered that the most musical note of their song should refuse to surface out of a throat so parched.

The daydreaming for cool days and even cooler nights on the part of a delirious city is combined with the act of constantly crushing tons of sugarcane for drinks. Green mangoes are mercilessly boiled by the kilo, skinned, pulped and crushed into yet another drink. This drink is a preventive measure against heatstroke. Dehydration is a grave danger during the months of May and June. That is why green lemons too come to the rescue of thirsty human beings. The juice of lemons is one of the most popular drinks at this time of the year, spiced as it is with a pinch of black salt and lots of sugar syrup.

I treat myself to a familiar drink as I remove the laced doily covering the glass jug filled with lemonade and placed on my writing table throughout the summer months. The doily is weighed down with a fringe of moonstones around its circumference and also helps to camouflage ugly marks made by time on the jug. I pour some more lemonade into a tall glass. It is reassuring to coil the fingers in-between the stem, leaves and petals of a rosebush that is carved wildly around the outer wall of the silver glass. I tighten my grip over the glass, a precious heirloom from a past fading away fast.

I wait for Bano Bua to cover her head with the pallu of her cotton sari before venturing out of the house to cross the Gomti, which has fishy waters but no fish.

As I sip lemonade, I also look beyond the screen woven from reeds of the scented *khas* plant put outside each window towards the start of every May. Before the blaze of the afternoon takes over, the screens are soaked in water in anticipation of the *loo.* The water-soaked *khas* screens halt and absorb the *loo* when it comes and cool it down.

Once the outdoors feel less like a furnace, the windows are thrown wide open. From my window I spy the sun preparing to finally call it a day. I watch the source of all life sink itself into a horizon decked in heavenly sheets patterned in pinks, purple and blood orange.

The city stirs after sunset. This is the price Lucknow must pay during the months of May and June for enjoying such radiant weather throughout the rest of the year.

The following day I wait for the muezzin to first finish his musical call to pray before throwing open the front door to welcome dawn.

On my way out I find that the flame from the candle, lit the previous dusk, has shrunk into a fatigued curl at its own feet, and I walk past it. I concentrate on the chorus created by an entire community of birds outside, and witness the face of dawn rosy with rest. Each strand of light shimmering at this hour is tousled.

The good morning puckers the mouth to blow me a kiss and some of that breath zips past by my cheek as if to wake me up too.

The solitary silhouette of a sage draped in saffron deeper than the colour of sunrise sails across the horizon. His humming halts outside the gate of our garden. Where he stands, the air is thick with the smoke of dried roots of sweet-smelling plants that soothe the soul, and are said to heal the body. The concoction carried by the sage smoulders in a bowl hanging from a chain that he swings with one hand. His other hand smartly lifts a trident in salutation. I join the palms of my hands and bow to honour the visitor.

I walk over to the gate to give the holy man everything my fist is able to fish out from my pocket, and also some fresh flowers plucked along the pathway. He accepts it all in a pouch slung across a shoulder. I am happy to hear him bless me and to wish me luck in-between mantras that he mumbles from behind a long but unkempt beard.

The clang of the bell of a cyclist distracts. It is probably the newspaper boy, who rolls up the day's news into many bundles of varying bulk and flings each subscription over the fences of different homes. The newspaper falls to the floor of each porch with a bored thud.

I also see the milkman swerve in and out of homes, balancing heavy aluminium pails in each hand. He continues to sail through many gates in the neighbourhood in rhythm to the "ding dong" of the bells that chime from the steeple of a church nearby, in a city that is home to Hindus, Muslims and Christians alike.

Bano Bua has dropped whatever she was doing in the house to shoot out of the front door like an arrow to target the vendor pushing his cart piled up with cucumbers. The echo of his sing-song jingles penetrates every corner of the lanes and alleys nearby, tempting one and all to tumble out of the summer slumber and buy the freshly plucked produce. It is promised to be more delicate than the fingers of Laila, crisp like the brittle rib of her emaciated lover and sweeter than the obsession that the two had for each other. The vegetable vendor, like every layman to landlord here, is familiar with Laila and Majnun, a popular legend of love and loss from the 12th century, brought to Lucknow by Persian travelers.

Bano Bua ignores the salesman's attempts to lace his trade talk with sensuality and poetry.

She reproaches him instead.

"What world do you think you live in? Do you seriously think that I will pay you the amount you ask for? Here, take this, you unfortunate one, and be quickly gone. I have other things to attend to," Bano Bua pouts.

"Why do you do this to me, Bua? Day after day you deprive me not only of cash but also of a smile. It will cost you nothing to say the same thing, but in kinder words, will it? Now look at your hand...it wilts in shame at the petty cash that you force it to hold," he pouts back.

"I have better things to do than to stand here listening to your lyrics and to your lies. Here is the money. Now give me the cucumbers and if I find a single maggot in the vegetables today, your brain is mincemeat when I see you tomorrow."

Then she is gone.

I picture Bano Bua pulling the end of the sari around her wisp waist and tucking it into the folds of the skirt across her flat stomach, for effect. She must grind her teeth too as she speaks, slanting her hand and waving it to make it look like a butcher's scalpel at the cheeky vendor standing on one leg and then on the other. He must wipe beads of sweat off his brow and suppress a smile behind the same metre-long cloth with red and white squares that he transforms into a wreath around the head to help him bear the heat of the day.

"Hai! The poor poet was so right when he said that it is impossible to delight in the sweet without having tasted the bitter," he sighs behind her back as she disappears inside the house. Slowly the vegetable vendor tows his trolley away and in a completely different pitch of voice, much higher than before, he returns to his hawking out of habit:

> My cucumbers are most green, they are crisp like Laila's fingers,
> They are very lean.
> Watch this one snap,
> Like the dream of lovers in their teens.
> Come and buy...Buy your cucumbers now,
> They are the best, I swear and I vow.

I wait at the front window for Bano Bua to finish sweeping the front yard before following her indoors for a cup of tea. But she has dropped the broomstick, a bouquet made from dozens of slim reeds dried, bound together and used to sweep away everything that is unwanted in life.

I hear her speak across the thick hedge of the henna bush to those across the street.

"The watermelon you sold me yesterday may look macho like yourself but it is less delicious than dried leaves," I hear her address someone, probably the fruit vendor.

I am quite familiar with her luscious vocabulary, but each time I hear Bano Bua say what she has just said I am prompted to cover both my ears with the hands. Bano Bua accuses the vendor of selling her fruit that is tasteless even before we have tasted it.

I was extremely embarrassed. I run indoors with the vendor's reply trailing off behind me.

"You must first make friends with the fruit to make it taste sweet, Bua. Now permit me to sell you something today. What should I offer you...?"

But Bano Bua has already lost interest in this man and moved on to her next victim, reminding the milkman that it is no longer milk that we seem to get from him, but water.

"No wonder the taps of Lucknow are running dry. It seems that the water of the river is the private property of your grandfather...the way you use it to dilute milk into nothing. Do you hear me, you rascal? Tell that father of yours that I can't wait to have a word with him...Go and tell the old man that his dream of trying to get rich by cheating me will collapse like a castle made of cards the day I decide to cast my curse upon all of you."

But the lad obviously does not care. He is used to suffering the bombastic, mostly benign blah-blah of the elderly and has learnt to ignore it. He hurries away to deliver milk to the next house with a big smile on his face, and without a word to Bano Bua.

VISION OF CLAUDE MARTIN AND GORI BIBI

To lock myself in the bathroom is to take a break from Bano Bua. I turn on the shower to maximum to shut out the noise from outside. This is a luxury I can afford only between 6 am and 8 am, the two hours when there is running water in the house. For the rest of the day, water is kept stored in the bathroom and in the kitchen in two gigantic buckets, one in red plastic and the other in blue. In fact, we grew up squatting on the floor of the bathroom to bathe by pouring water collected in buckets over ourselves with a mug. But later in life I spent so much time sitting at home that it seemed like a good idea to install a shower in the bathroom so that I could stand beneath it.

Once upon a time, I remember, the buckets and the gigantic vessels filled with water in the bathroom came in copper. It is difficult to say when and how the copper vessels disappeared to be replaced by plastic. If the monsoons are delayed again this year there will be even less water in the city. The thought makes me really splash water on that morning.

At first the image is blurred behind the downpour but a nose that resembles a parrot's beak below a broad forehead floats before me. The smile radiating out of a face framed by a periwig from the 18th century is European. Having lowered my look to other parts of the apparition, I see that the visitant is dressed in a regimental navy-blue uniform, decorated with gold braids and epaulettes.

Then I am humming.

> May our founder's name endure ever spotless, ever pure!
> Hail! Hail the name we own,
> Hail to the giver.
> Blessing and bright renown,
> Be his forever!
> All his martial deed may die lasting still his charity,
> This his laurels for aye,
> Dead he lives in us today,
> This then our song shall be as we chant his eulogy...

The one on my mind is the French Maj. Gen. Claude Martin, founder of two La Martiniere schools in Lucknow, one in Kolkata and another in his native Lyon. And the tune playing in my head is the school song, which we sang annually on 13 September with more gusto than we sang the national anthem. On this day in 1800, Martin died in Lucknow, and it is observed as Founder's Day by the students of both La Martiniere Girls' at Khurshid Manzil, and Constantia, the quaint mausoleum that Martin built for himself and is now a college for boys. Memory makes me smile but I stop myself. For I was brought up on the belief that only people who are crazy chuckle while alone.

On Founder's Day, the girls wore white frocks, black leather shoes and white nylon socks. The boys came in khaki pants and shirts, with the silk of their navy blue ties gleaming gloriously. In the auditorium, the evening always started with dances from around the world and with one drama in several acts, put up by the students. The performance took place against the background of a painting of the school coat of arms. The images on the coat of arms tell a tidy tale of Martin's life in Lucknow.

Designed by Martin, at the centre of the emblem is a shield, with a picture of seven flags, each bearing a fish symbolic of Martin's relationship with the rulers of Lucknow. The ship is for Martin's journey to India from Lyon, the French city, represented by a lion and pronounced by us like the name of the animal. The setting sun depicts the last days of Martin, the city's most romantic resident from the second half of the 18th century.

In the winter months, when the temperature in Lucknow can dip down to zero degrees Celsius, we wore navy blue blazers to school with Martin's coat of arms embossed on the pocket above the left breast, with *Labore et Constantia* embroidered below. While in school I was not sure what the Latin words meant, but now I know where I first learnt to appreciate the spirit of toil (*labore*) and fidelity (*constantia*).

It was at an event organised on Founder's Day that I watched a performance by Ramesh, who had eyes that slant like those of people from East Asia. Ramesh is the son of Captain Ram Singh Thakur, bandmaster of the official orchestra of the armed forces. Ramesh is remembered for performing the moonwalk on stage, two decades before that out-of-this-world dance step rocketed

Michael Jackson to stardom. When we became friends, Ramesh had us gaping at him in yet more admiration as he told us that his father, from the eleventh Gorkha Rifles of the Indian Army, had composed the tune for the country's national anthem.

The Founder's Day feast after the performance offered the students biryani, the saffron-rice delicacy layered in goat's meat and leavened bread baked in a clay oven. The meals were eaten with a fork and knife on long tables with students already divided into four competing houses of the school, each house represented by a different colour and motto. I was in Cornwallis House and went to the table laid out in green crockery, with the motto "Never Give In" forever on my mind. Joan, my best friend, and I were otherwise inseparable, but she made her way to Lyon House in yellow, where the motto practiced was "Perseverance Conquers All". The student from La Martiniere Boys' College, whom I had been admiring secretly for a whole year, was wrenched away from my vision and seated on the table for those in Hudson House in red. The motto there was "Do or Die". The fourth house was named after Martin, its flag blue, and the motto "Never Despair".

The Founder's Day celebrations closed with a dance party that was supervised by teachers who rarely smiled. They watched every move made by the students and marched up and down the wooden dance floor with hands behind their back, making sure that the lights were turned off at the first stroke of midnight. This was perhaps the only occasion when the boys from Constantia and the girls from Khurshid Manzil who had secretly exchanged rings and love letters actually got to hold each other for a few hours. Here they were tempted, but did not dare to dance cheek to cheek to the Cliff Richards number 'Evergreen Tree'.

During Martin's lifetime, the same room was used as a library, with 4,000 volumes of reading material in Greek, Latin, Sanskrit, Persian and English, and an amazing collection of paintings. Today it is stripped of all its treasures, including the French chandeliers.

Martin was one among a large group of Europeans who came to Lucknow to get rich. There were the Portuguese, Spanish and Italians, who came as traders. Martin made his money and also a home in Lucknow, where he lived for over two decades with his many mistresses. He was born in 1735 in southern Lyon, at a time when interest in South Asia was at its peak in Europe. As a teenager he enlisted with the French East India Company to be a soldier in India. He arrived in Pondicherry in 1752. He was lucky to escape a sinking ship off the coast of Madras in 1761. Then he had walked all the way to Kolkata to find a job with the army of the British East India Company.

Kolkata at that time was a new town founded by the English on land leased from Emperor Aurangzeb. The English were no longer just traders but king makers. Martin was employed as a revenue collector and travelled for work to the countryside on behalf of the British. In Lucknow, Martin sold military equipment to the ruler, and after he had earned enough money, he bought property. He was made superintendent of the Lucknow Arsenal and in 1794 led a cavalry against the rebellious Rohila Pathans in Avadh.

Martin became wealthy by providing European goods and services to the ruling family and eventually gave up the idea of returning to his place of birth. He got news that France was not safe to live in after the Revolution in 1789. He was saddened by the news of the violent death of Antoine Polier, his long-time architect friend, in 1795.

After making his money in Lucknow, Polier had returned to France only to be brutally murdered at Avignon. He lived in France with his wife and daughters but was killed, in all probability by those jealous of the wealth he had brought back from India. His house was set on fire, his wife burnt alive and his daughters raped. When Martin got this news he decided to remain in Lucknow.

His life in Lucknow began in Lakhipeera, the place with one lakh trees. This was rented accommodation. Soon, he could afford several homes on the hill overlooking the Gomti. He owned a covered market below the Lakshman Tila and the collection from all this property was significant. He designed the lavish Farhat Baksh as his home, where he lived like a *laatsaheb*, a local lord with many mistresses and adopted children. Joseph Queiros was his Spanish housekeeper who, along with the Qadri brothers, took care of Martin's many properties. Farhat Baksh was full of European treasures, displaying a perfect museum of infinite amusement. Some of this glory is reflected in Constantia, perhaps the largest European funerary in India. Martin willed that, after his death, Constantia would be used as a college for instructing men in the English language, and that his tomb be well kept. Constantia continues to intrigue citizens and visitors alike about the city.

In the 19th century, W.H. Russell, a war correspondent for *The Times*, wrote that Constantia was the most curious structure he ever saw:

> At first glance one exclaims, how beautiful! What a splendid building! At the second glance the response is that it must have been built by a madman with its eccentric array of statues, the huge lions' heads, the incongruous columns, arches, pillars, windows and flights of stairs leading to nothing, which are the distinguishing features of the Constantia now La Maritinere College.

Out of the many women Martin loved, Boulone Lise was a favourite. Martin felt that luck had made her fall to his lot. The daughter of Nawab Fazal Khan Bahadur, grandson of the Vizier to Emperor Aurangzeb, Boulone Lise was born in 1766 and joined Martin's household when she was about nine years old. She was nicknamed Gori Bibi or "The Fair-Skinned Mistress".

Martin wanted his property to be given to her. He said that, for her, he had the greatest regard and affection. He found her worthy of gratitude for the services rendered to him. Out of deference for the customs of Lucknow society, and mindful of the prevalent purdah system, he also desired that when Boulone Lise and his other mistresses visited his tomb, every man would be drawn away from the house.

Boulone Lise was a child bride, and also a victim of domestic violence. She was rescued by Martin and grew up pledging eternal gratitude and love to her benefactor. She was a widow longer than she was a bride. The mother of an adopted son, she remained the matriarch who controlled the affairs of Martin's household from the confines of the zenana, or ladies quarters, after he passed away.

Martin mentions her lovingly and with great respect in his will, leaving instructions for her care and well-being after his death, and for a tomb to be constructed for her near him.

In fact, Martin made generous provisions for each of the seven women in his life, two of them sisters, and especially for his most amiable girl, Boulone. All these women outlived Martin.

Compared to Constantia, the tomb of Boulone Lise is simple. It is an elevated square structure in one corner of the sprawling premises of Constantia, and lay hidden behind a forest of vegetation till recently.

The forest around the mausoleum of Boulone Lise has now been cleared. After it was discovered that the wooden rafters supporting the terrace above the plinth were made hollow by termites and dampness, renovation work was started. The finials needed to be fired with copper to provide the distinctive green colour and were reconstructed on a potter's wheel, then placed in a kiln to replicate the original process.

The delicate and intricate latticework is painstakingly handmade rather than machine moulded. Dampness, the cause for perennial exasperation of old buildings near the river, is controlled by using modern methods. Now a garden surrounds the elegant standalone structure that is seen here as a symbol of true love.

Bano Bua points out that there are in fact three "Taj Mahals" or monuments of love in Lucknow. One is the sparkling white and pistachio-green tomb of Boulone Lise. The other two are tombs of Saadat Ali Khan II, ruler of Lucknow till 1814, and Khurshidzadi, his most beloved wife.

This Saadat Ali Khan built a home in 1810 for Khurshidzadi. He called it Khurshid Manzil and designed it to resemble a French fortress in imitation of the home of Martin. Khurshid Manzil is on two floors with six turrets on the roof and four gates with drawbridges over a moat around it. The staircase is built indoors as it was used only by women, who lived in a world of their own. But before Khurshid Manzil was finished, Khurshidzadi died. Saadat Ali Khan died soon after. He was betrayed by people he thought had cared for him. The king was in pain from ulcers caused by problems of the liver. One day his favourite son-in-law offered him a bowl of soup, poisoned with the juice of a chameleon that he had hunted and crushed with his own hands. On the king's sudden death, Khurshid Manzil became the home of Badshah Begum, his departed majesty's temperamental daughter-in-law. This queen had physically attacked her husband, pulling at his beard and tearing his clothes. When the childless queen realised that a maidservant was expecting her husband's child, she got the pregnant woman murdered, making sure that His Majesty went to his grave without being cheered for having left an heir, but not from her.

These tales of the murdered maidservant were told to us by our sadistic seniors in school. They had convinced us that the blood-curdling cries of the murdered woman's ghost were heard to this day. We listened to similar ghost stories without moving in our respective beds in the school dormitory, often in a pool of urine, too frightened to go to the toilet in the middle of the night.

There was also the ghost of Constantia, said to be the sweetheart Martin left behind in Lyon, France. She was the lady in a blue dress who descended down from heaven to look for her lost engagement ring on the terrace adjacent to the dormitory on nights when the moon was full.

The most hair-raising story of them all was told after the teacher on duty had switched off the light at 9 pm and retired to the staff quarters. We were told by senior students to be quiet if we wanted to listen to the voices of men groan in pain and to the chain of the prisoners as it clanged its way up to the first floor of Khurshid Manzil, on the same staircase that we had used only an hour earlier. We would even sneak out of bed to huddle near the gigantic door closed from the outside, trying not to breathe so that we could hear the ghosts better. Once we could take it no more we ran back into bed, with a few of us disappearing under the quilt of another person.

After the 1857 war between Indians and the British-Indian Army was won by the British, Khurshid Manzil was converted into a mess for soldiers. It was here that Sir Henry Havelock, Sir James Outram and Sir Colin Campbell met on 17 November 1857, covered in the dust of battle. With the walls of the castle still reverberating with the din of gunshots of Indian freedom fighters, they shook hands and vowed under the roof of my alma mater to keep Lucknow safe from the local rebels. However, a little hesitant to proselytise so soon after a near defeat of the British, Christian missionaries diverted their zeal to educate people instead. A grant from Martin's fund allowed Khurshid Manzil to be used for education purposes in 1867, with Mrs Abbot as the first principal of La Martiniere Girls' High School.

THE ANGLO-INDIANS

The presence of Europeans like Claude Martin and Gori Bibi gave birth to a new community of Eurasians, or people popularly known as Anglo-Indians.

The first European traders were the Portuguese in 1510. The Dutch came in the early 17th century and the French later in the same century. The British survived the other Europeans after Robert Clive, a British East India Company clerk, defeated the French and the Indian princes in a 1757 battle. After that victory, the British felt that they owned the entire Indian subcontinent and established major settlements in Mumbai, Chennai and Kolkata.

In the late 18th and early 19th centuries, British officers and soldiers were allowed to take local wives, and their children grew up to man the railways, telegraph services, postal services, customs services, hospitals and schools. They were officers in the police and in the military.

In Lucknow many Anglo-Indian families lived in Lawrence Terrace, also called Chaupar, where Saadat Ali Khan II, perhaps the most able ruler of Lucknow, had the royal stables. In the early 19th century, some commercial activities were shifted away from the overcrowded old city with narrow lanes to a new location near Chaupar in Hazratgunj. This was a handsome street till 1844, with a neat range of shops on each side, all of the same height, with piazzas along the front. Hazratgunj soon shrunk into a narrow lane sandwiched between ungainly structures, making it impossible for an elephant or camel to pass through.

When the British took over Lucknow in 1857, they revamped Hazratgunj into a broad avenue with wide pavements, shaded with tall trees to resemble London's Oxford Street. The cross-shaped building of the Chaupar stables was converted into barracks for the 32nd Regiment, and the Lucknow Club came up next to it as a place for the amusement of officers and gentlemen. The low, long structure, made from one lakh bricks, each brick known locally as *lakhori*, stood out for its milky white walls, washed regularly in paste made from powdered lentils, shells, sugarcane, and lime extract, and churned into *chunam* to give it a marble-like shimmer. Inside, the main hall is still fitted with a wooden floor that was regularly polished and powdered in the past. After independence, the Lucknow Club was opened for use by civilians.

During the dance organised to select a May Queen, and at the New Year party, we would rock and roll to recorded music made by the Lucknow-born Sir Cliff Richards and Elvis Presley.

Today tears of slime run down the discoloured walls of the Lucknow Club, where men too ashamed to drink alcohol at home sit in semi-darkness to gamble as well as to play a game of cards for long hours with other men.

After the British left in 1947, the barracks were converted into homes for Anglo-Indian families. Later, the city municipality pulled down the massive mud walls of the royal stables to line the street with two rows of modest double-storey flats. The buildings were painted in yellow, with little gardens in front of each house on the ground floor, shaded by majestic trees on the pavement. The ambience around Lawrence Terrace reflected a little of the courtly life of yesteryear as well as the more modern, socialist spirit of post-independent India. The colony got its name from Sir Henry Lawrence, a British resident who is buried at the Residency, now a public park, below the inscription: "Here lies Henry Lawrence, who tried to do his duty".

My Anglo-Indian friends Mildred Cline and Maxine Cline lived here, and I went to church with them, learning to sing Christmas carols better than them. The houses were comfortable but not large, so the road in-between the spotlessly clean pavements outside was just fine for endless games of hide-and-seek and for cycling up and down for hours. When I was a teenager the evenings were often spent *gunjing* in shocking pink miniskirts; the dream was to match the Twiggy-inspired outfit with a tall pair of Nancy Sinatra boots when out to watch a film at the Mayfair cinema. It was not unusual to begin a Sunday with a morning film show at Mayfair, where David Solomon sang 'Happy Birthday to You' in his baritone voice for all those in the audience who had their birthdays that week. A cake came to add to the celebrations from the Kwality Restaurant on the ground floor. Sunday evenings were spent queuing up for a softie ice-cream sold opposite the grand General Post Office.

All high summer afternoon dates were at the air-conditioned British Council Library. The winter months were idyllic for practicing hockey on the sprawling sports field of Lucknow University under the expert guidance of Olympic player Bula Ganguly. There was so much that I managed to get out of growing up in Lucknow apart from eating *tundey* kebabs. I took singing lessons at the Bhatkhande College of Music and cycled down before the crack of dawn to the Sharma Yoga School below the Monkey Bridge. My father had made a conscious decision to move the family out of the Muslim environs of the old city on Nadan Mahal Road and to make a home near the more cosmopolitan neighbourhood of Hazratgunj.

The Indian Coffee House on Ashok Marg was managed by a South Indian cooperative society and it was my journalist and politician father's second home. It was a treat to be occasionally invited by him to a delicious plate of dosa there, often in the company of poets and politicians. Those were the days when legislatures did not hide behind bulletproof vests, and mingled freely with those who had voted them to power.

I learnt to swim at La Martiniere Girls' School, where I recall cutting many a record. I cut another record as the only student in class seven to earn a zero in arithmetic in the entire history of the school. The memory of the shrill voice of class teacher Mrs Cook returns to warn me that I would get nowhere in life with such bad grades in class. Mrs Cook was aghast when I told her in class five that the only ambition I had was to seek out the mouth of the tunnel hidden inside the moat surrounding the principal's office and to journey across the darkness and the dirt in search of a favourite student at the boys' La Martiniere College. Eventually the magic of Mohini Manglik in the postgraduate block of Lucknow University worked miracles as she made her students fall in love with English Literature. Those were also the days when it was quite possible to educate oneself on the once-wondrous campus of Lucknow University, where the library was a favourite haunt of some of us. The campus is overcrowded and tension between student leaders and the university administration often turns ugly these days, discouraging female students to spend time on the campus in the library or on the sports field.

"Why don't you go to the British Council library anymore?" Bano Bua wants to know.

"Bua, the British Council library does not exist anymore. The place is a travel agency now."

"What? A travel agency? And since when did books decide to travel?"

It just felt nice to participate in silly talk sometimes, so I continued with a giggle, "Bua, it is not books that travel, but people."

"Who would want to ever leave Lucknow? On the other hand, I can't think of anyone wanting to come here either."

I was not sure whether Bano Bua, whose untiring tongue has an opinion on its tip on everything under the sky, was joking when she said that. Come to think of it, who indeed would want to visit a people who remain so very partial to the past that they orphan the present and the future seems nowhere in their thought.

Despite what the bright brochures say about Lucknow being a city of gardens and of culture, the fact is that citizens do not know what to do with their garbage seen littered all over the roadside. In Lucknow we do not know what to do with some of our finest monuments either, except to demolish many and to use the same premises for crass constructions. Many tears were shed when the stately low roof of the Pioneer Press building from 1933 conceived by Walter Burley Griffin, a student of Frank Lloyd Wright, was pulled down in recent times to make room for a modern high-rise building that remains a carbuncle on one side of the otherwise grand Vidhan Sabha Marg. It was at *The Pioneer* that I learnt how to best use the English language from the editor, S.N. Ghosh. Cub reporters were never allowed to forget at *The Pioneer,* the newspaper that started in 1865, that it had once employed Rudyard Kipling, Winston Churchill and Desmond Young as writers.

The culture of the city is changing as well. The violence on the streets is appalling.

It is awful the way Aunty Joyce Carter was murdered in her own living room in Lawrence Terrace. Nina Solomon and I were often invited by Aunty Carter to share the goodies she brought from her frequent trips abroad. She regaled us with tales of far and near. And for being with her for as long as she wanted us to, we were rewarded with cheese cubes from Holland and bars of chocolate picked up in England. We could not help but notice how Aunty had tried to lighten her dark skin with face powder, and every evening she wore a clean cotton dress with big flowers and matching shoes. A handbag dangled down her arm as she strolled towards Hazratgunj. It is called *gunjing* to saunter in Hazratgunj, which is not just a market, but a place to see and to be seen, to exchange pleasantries with others without having to get intimate with anyone, to lounge at Kwality's or Benbows for a pastry, or to relax at the Royal Cafe with a drink while a live band plays music on weekends. Before independence in 1947, when the British were still in the city, dogs and Indians were not allowed on the mile-long Hazratgunj, flanked then by elegant shops with glass doors fitted with bells, restaurants and a cinema house called Mayfair. Two grand gateways at each end had cordoned off the marketplace from Indians once.

Bano Bua was certain that Aunty Carter's ancestor, Mr Ramble, was actually a dark-skinned gentleman called Rambali. He had converted to Christianity and someone in the family married a European. That is why Aunty was swarthy while her son was tall and fair, just like an Englishman, insisted Bano Bua when she was in the mood for some gossip.

Sometime in the 1980s Aunty Carter was visited by a stranger who asked her to vacate her home because he wanted to move in. A certain amount of money was offered to her to do so, but she refused. Late one evening the septuagenarian aunty opened her front door to find out who had knocked, and was instantly struck on the head with something hard. She slumped to the floor after that blow, and like the flickering end of a burnt out candle she was there one moment and gone in the next. This is just like thousands of other Anglo-Indian families who had once dominated life in the city but out of fear and insecurity had suddenly migrated almost en masse during the 1960s in particular to faraway places like Australia, Canada and England after the British left India in 1947.

Now I wait for Bano Bua to oil the creaking door generously with grease meant for Singer sewing machines, and bought from a shop once run by ladies with moonlight-pale skin and gently stooping shoulders. The ladies at the Singer sewing machine shop were Parsi, from the city's tiny Zoroastrian community. Their shop no longer exists, but once the Singer Merritt and Pfaff showroom in Hazratgunj was chic. This shop was so intimidatingly upmarket that Bano Bua had felt too shabby and embarrassed to visit it. Whatever she required to be able to continue her constant sewing and embroidering, she would request my grandmother or Aunty Nigam to get for her from any shop in Hazratgunj.

In fact, the first Parsis came to Avadh precisely because the markets in Lucknow were so smart. Perhaps one of the first to come was Nawrojee Damakawala, with a chest full of pearls and bundles of exotic pieces of silk. The story goes that Damakawala had thundered into the city on an Arab steed one day. This was in the 19th century and Damakawala had a personal invitation from Mohammed Ali Shah, who ruled Avadh till 1842. His Majesty, you see, had heard of a pearl that Damakawala had in his collection that he longed to possess for a special ring he wore on the third finger of his left hand.

Once in the city, Damakawala did such roaring business that he stayed on to build a home in the most expensive corner of Hazratgunj. When the demand for pearls slackened, Damakawala diversified into transportation and hospitality. He launched a horse carriage manufacturing business and littered the streets of Lucknow with buggies and carriages of different shapes and sizes. He ran the Prince of Wales Hotel in the vicinity of Hazratgunj and when the time came he was the first to open an automobile showroom there.

Many Zoroastrian families, like the ancestors of Damakawala, had sailed out of Persia in the 8th century to escape persecution, and to safeguard their faith. Those who migrated to South Asia settled mainly in Gujarat and Sind and in coastal cities like Mumbai, where some of them gradually worked their way up, mostly as merchants to enjoy great fame and fortune. Later Parsi businessmen spread around the Indian peninsula.

In the 19th century, Hazratgunj was lined with shops run by some affluent Parsis. There was Minoo & Dinshaw, selling the fanciest watches, clocks and silverware. Sohrabjee Debus was in the liquor business and the wine he had on display is remembered as better than the best. None of these shops exist anymore as Minoo & Dinshaw is a bookshop now and the population of Parsis in Lucknow has shrunk to about 17 families.

Along with all the people of Afghan, Arab, Chinese, Dravidian, European, Mongol, Turkic, Slavic and other origins that I grew up with in Lucknow, I had a Parsi friend. But I lost touch with Sheila Dinshaw a long time ago and know not if she belongs to the family of Dinshaw Ice Cream distributors, or Minoo & Dinshaw booksellers in Lucknow. At that age in life, Sheila was simply a friend. I did not see her as a Parsi, and felt no need to find out more about her elders. Now that I have discovered what a delicious melting pot of different people and cultures Lucknow has always been, I wish I knew where to find Sheila so that she could tell me more about herself.

MORNING WALK

It is routine for us to walk down to Sikandar Bagh at the crack of as many dawns as possible. But this morning I had lost too much time staring at dawn.

It was already sweltering. Pity about the no walk this morning. It is always nice to kick away the walking shoes bought from Bata and to soak the naked feet in dew, laid out like a carpet on the lawns of Sikandar Bagh. We always walk briskly for 45 minutes in silence, and only after that is Bano Bua allowed to continue her chatter.

We usually pause below the most majestic *peepal* tree among many others in the garden and I plead with Bano Bua to repeat at least one of the legends from Sikandar Bagh.

"I will, but here, have some of this first," Bano Bua says, digging into a little basket that she brings with her during our walk. She pulls out a custard apple, a tiny guava, or a fistful of *falsa,* the delightful mauve berries from the basket. If it is a mango no bigger than the palm of my hand then it is massaged in a gentle, circular motion till Bano Bua is sure that the pulp inside has separated from the seed. I am given the fruit to bite and to spit away the black seal at the mouth of the mango, before sucking out the juice leisurely as I listen to Bano Bua.

She was 15 years old when Wajid Ali Shah, the last ruler of Avadh, first heard her song. Then he asked to see her. When he did, he could not stop poetry from gushing out of his soul quicker than rivers from a glacier. The raising and lowering of her eyelashes felt like someone stabbing a knife into him. When she looked at him, he saw her eyes brimming over with intoxicants, tempting him to sip. As for her heart-shaped face, it was an open book of longing and love. Such was the beauty of Sadarun Nisa, named Sikandar Mahal by Wajid Ali Shah.

His Majesty loved her at first sight and later he married her.

Sikandar Mahal was lovely to know. Her slaves adored her as much as her lord and master. The king built for her a palace with an entrance imagined as one more glorious than the gates of heaven.

Look carefully at the ruins of the gate gilded with floral designs that make even the most exquisite embroidery on gossamer like garments fold away in shame. More than 150 years ago, the walled enclosure was laid out with flower beds and fountains to match the Garden of Eden, and Sikandar Mahal lived in a two-storey palace patterned in a Grecian style. Ruins of this palace are still there, as if in weeping memory of a mistress no more.

Wajid Ali Shah was dethroned by the British after eight years on the throne of Avadh. When he was forced to leave Lucknow for Kolkata, Sikandar Mahal lived up to the title given to her in honour of Alexander, the great Greek conqueror, who is called Sikandar in Urdu.

Sikandar Mahal refused to wilt in grief. She got her staff to train as soldiers, converting Sikandar Bagh overnight from a palace of pleasure into a barrack of militants. Men, women and eunuchs alike kicked away numerous bells tied around their ankles. Musical instruments were replaced with batons and rifles, secretly given to them by rebellious Indian soldiers in the British Army. None had time for song and dance anymore, as everyone prepared to beat the British out of Lucknow in 1857.

Sadly Sikandar Mahal did not live to see her people take up arms against the British. After her sudden death, her slaves kept her spirit alive and joined forces with soldiers sent by Bahadur Shah Zafar, the last Mughal emperor of Delhi, to engage in the first war of independence against the British.

In November 1857, Hindus washed themselves in holy water, Muslims swore on the Koran and together they took a vow to give the British a good run for their money.

After a ferocious fight that lasted for nearly 10 months, the battle was, alas, won by the British. In the struggle for freedom thousands of Indians died, but not before both civilians and rebellious soldiers had frightened the daylight out of the foreigners. During numerous encounters in the city where every nook and cranny was turned into a battlefield, many fought the enemy fist to fist, like wild cats. That time the grass was sprayed with a deep red colour from the blood of human beings trying to kill each other.

This was Bano Bua's dramatic conclusion as she wiped a tear or two, as well as beads of sweat, from her face.

I love this story by Bano Bua that Hindus and Muslims had united to fight in the 1857 uprising against the British. What she does not tell or perhaps is not aware of is the other side of the story about many Hindu, Muslim and Sikh people who had also helped the British to fight Indians and protected the interest of the East India Company in Avadh. Another great story about a woman engaged in battle against the British at Sikandar Bagh is about Uda Bai. A courageous slave of Sikandar Mahal, Uda Bai had slipped into green garments and concealed herself on the tallest branch of the biggest *peepal* tree in the garden.

And from her place in hiding, Uda Bai had aimed and shot, then aimed and shot again, killing at least six enemy soldiers. One bullet bounced off a soldier she killed to pierce the thigh of Sir Colin Campbell, a British commander. He was in such pain and so angry at being hit by the enemy that he ordered the walls of Sikandar Bagh, despite their immense beauty, to be bombarded till they crumbled into dust.

Uda Bai was eventually discovered and shot. It was only after her body crashed to the ground from the tree did the gallant officers and gentlemen realise that the brave sniper was a woman.

I get goosebumps at the thought that perhaps Uda Bai was atop the same tree that I always choose to stand under after my walk in the morning around Sikandar Bagh. In that horrible clash, nearly 2,000 Indians were killed by the British, who decided to demolish the imperial city of Lucknow indiscriminately. After the battle was over and the British had won Avadh, they washed their hands and sins in the Gomti, which seems to have been more generous with its waters then than it is now.

The whole of Sikandar Bagh was dismantled by the new lords of the city. The gorgeous garden was parted into two smaller premises, with a thoroughfare of brick and mortar paved in the middle over the bed of numerous flowers and herbs. After the city was redesigned by the British, the gates of Sikandar Bagh were opened to the public for use as a park. The place is now the home of the National Botanical Gardens. Come to think of it, it has been a while since we last went to Sikandar Bagh, which is so overcrowded these days. All of Lucknow seems to come here in search of Nature's bounties.

Look at the crowd of people who have made a garbage can of every corner of Lucknow and now comb the city for fresh air and open skies. I long to be away from this crowd and at the premises of the Taj instead. This is a hotel building painted in white and spread over 33 acres of gardens. It is landscaped like a lovely little paradise beside the river. I love the snow-white architecture of the hotel, which has such a sweeping sense of space. It is perhaps the first building in post-independent Lucknow to match the aesthetics and grandeur of construction that had taken place routinely in Lucknow in the past. It is built in marble and fitted with tall windows and doors adorned with glass to welcome a generous amount of sunshine into its air-conditioned interior.

Once in a while I drag Bano Bua to the Sahib Cafe for a cup of coffee that is not worth its price, but just an excuse to enjoy the luxurious ambience. Then, Bano Bua always sits on the edge of the silk-lined chair in hilarious discomfort, almost all of her face covered with one end of her muslin shawl.

She is too shy to drink the coffee I insist on offering her; she says she will not touch it because the cup it is served in does not belong to her. Besides, it is tea, brewed by herself in her own cup and garnished with a pinch of salt apart from the usual milk and sugar, that she reminds me is her favourite drink. Not coffee.

At this five-star hotel, Bano Bua is always at her quiet best. After a while of watching Bano Bua sitting so quietly I want to give her a hug.

Once in a while I do enjoy the delicious feeling of utter contentment found within the confines of a cuddle from Bano Bua. I want nothing more then. I rock against Bano Bua's swaying body, basking in her undying love for me. My head barely rests on her flat chest, too afraid to do anything more than that to her frail frame. Her bones are brittle, and crackle like dry wood in a fireplace every time she bends down to roll out the bamboo mat and spread the prayer rug over it to face Mecca five times a day. And each time that she bows, prostrates herself, and stands up again in answer to the call to prayer, her joints creak. Then I wince at the thought that one day I might see her snap before me. I imagine her reduced to a heap of twigs collected from the wilderness surrounding the Dilkusha Palace, now abandoned, and its ruins rumoured to be haunted by the memory of all those who have loved and lived here, from Vishnu worshippers to Europeans.

The Dilkusha was once a grand hunting lodge, designed in the early 19th century by Sir Gore Ousely in imitation of Seaton Delvel to nurse his nostalgia for Northumberland, and to delight the heart of Muslim princes of Persian origin, fond of hunting deer in Lucknow. Once real hunters had made Dilkusha their home. Later, when rulers fell into decadence and indulged in jamboree more than governance, hunting in the real sense was considered a bother. So the forest surrounding Dilkusha was shaved and manicured. The place was landscaped to look like an imitation of wilderness with an artificial lake. All game was first tamed so that royalty could shoot an obedient flock of birds or an animal from the comfort of a couch, if indeed that happened to be the wish of the day. To witness this game, pretty women were trained to waltz in praise of the aristocracy's great sportsmanship. Some 49 professionals divided into seven groups of seven dancers were always at hand at Dilkusha to cheer on His Majesty. Each group of dancers was dressed in seven different colours and made a pirouette on cue after the fall of every bird by His Majesty.

NARESH THE RICKSHAWALA

I wait for Naresh to cycle the rickshaw up to the front gate and brake. I watch him look around before getting off the driver's seat. It takes a few seconds for him to steady himself on his feet. He rattles the tongue of the round, metal bell attached to the handlebar of the rickshaw on his right to announce his arrival. Then he pats his greasy hair into place and settles the scarf of cheap cotton cloth back on his shoulder. When none of us emerge from the house, he takes a few steps back to the rickshaw and climbs into the basin meant for passengers to rest their feet, just below the plastic-covered seat in a gaudy colour and made comfortable with thick straw stuffing. He bends his dhoti-clad legs into a haunch and sits down. Pulling out packets from the pocket of his knee-length shirt, he strikes a stick against a matchbox till the chemical-tipped wood is lit. With great care he brings the flame close to the hand-rolled tobacco he is already balancing in-between the lips. As the tobacco lights up he inhales the smoke deep, sparking off a sudden fountain of light at the burning end of his wicked but divine-smelling cigar, made in India. When he sucks at the tobacco again, the fire brightens up the space around his face once more, as if he is in the presence of a gorgeous glow-worm.

Through the smoke, I imagine Naresh also humming under his breath one of the numerous four-line ballads he keeps bringing back from the nautanki, the folk theatre performances that sail seasonally from suburb to suburb. Naresh is highly popular, playing parts in the annual Ramlila productions held outdoors before large audiences, narrating adventures from the life of Lord Rama, king of the ancient Suryavanshi rulers of Ayodhya.

But Naresh feels most at home while performing in the nautanki mainly because there he does not have to bother with religious moralising. The nautanki performances revolve mostly around the universal themes of love, loss and laughter that resonate with all human beings. Everyone wanted Naresh to go to school and not to the nautanki. They tried to get him to prepare for a job in the army or the police department or even at a shop in the nearest marketplace, but Naresh spent his entire youth sleeping during the day. In the evening he washed and massaged himself with a fist full of pungent-smelling oil extracted from the chameli flower. He stood for a split second before the mirror to make sure that the sooty blue *soorma* powder flicked up by the tip of the little finger of his right hand and flecked across the inside of first the right and then the left eye was in place. After that he was ready to hop back on the rickshaw to pedal towards the periphery of the city for yet another romp at the nautanki.

His head was always full of loud music and he muttered to himself lines from the exaggerated dialogues he delivered on stage. He was always ready to enjoy the same silly humour so popular with nautanki audiences as well as actors like him. The least of his worries was his next meal. During the nautanki season he always ate with the cast on the ground where performances were held under a tent. He would leave the premises in the wee hours of the morning only after having his fill of jalebis made from white batter, deep-fried and soaked in a rich syrup that was a mixture of sugar, a drop of rose water and warm milk. What preoccupied him most of the time was the fear that he may never get to play the role of Laila in this lifetime.

Laila and Majnun is a story, originally from Persia, about unfulfilled love, and is second in popularity only to the other great drama about love and loss, called *Taramati and Raja Harishchandra.* The Persian tale of Laila-Majnun is Indianised and shows the lovers living in Sindh and buried in the Rajasthani village of Binjaur village near Anupgarh, where an annual five-day fair is held every June, attracting numerous couples, who come here in memory of the star-crossed lovers.

As time passes by the likelihood of Naresh playing Laila indeed dims. His steadily expanding girth will soon prevent him from doing justice to the scrawny memory of Laila. However, Naresh has other qualities required by an actor to play Laila, like a clear complexion, a delicate enough physique, and of course the passion to desperately want to play female roles. It is his voice that is a problem.

Naresh may look effeminate but he can never sound like a woman. When Naresh sings his voice roars louder than the drums rolling in the wings during performances. He was born with a natural sense of music. His singing has astounding range and a breathless depth that inspires director after director year after year to cast him as the fearless martyr Shaheed Bhagat Singh, executed for his patriotism by the British. Much to his frustration, Naresh feels that he has been typecast. He has played Bhagat Singh so often on stage that the entire crew calls him Shaheed or "martyr". But the patient and good-natured Naresh has not given up his dream of playing Laila one day. He spends a lot of his spare time trying to tone down the alto in his majestic voice to a scale that sounds a little more like a soprano.

I have known Naresh since forever. I was three years old when I started kindergarten at La Martiniere Girls' School. It was a much slimmer Naresh who collected five other students in a rickshaw to pedal us all, ever so gently, to and back from school for more than a decade. In-between, he slept somewhere in the row of five rooms built for household help, beyond the backyard of the family villa. The story goes that a day before his ninth birthday he had sleepwalked to the big banyan tree still standing before our house, and claimed an abandoned bicycle parked beside the trunk. Naresh had never been seen cycling before, but he rode this one non-stop and round and round the white cows with the chipped horns. As for the cows, they could not have cared less, and continued to stare beyond him, chewing on plastic bags from the refuge that spills out of all the disposal enclosures put up with such responsibility by the city municipal board. This spectacle put up by Naresh took place at midday at the tail end of one June, when temperatures had reached over 40 degrees Celsius. Despite the searing heat,

Naresh's marathon attracted a crowd that stayed on to cheer when he rounded off his circuiting with a collapse to the ground exactly as the sun dipped below the horizon. That same night an army of dark clouds thundered over the heavens quite out of the blue to drench the plains and people with a rainfall that lasted all night long. The morning saw Jumman, an elderly rickshaw puller in the neighbourhood, never wake up from sleep. Those who remembered the magnificent cycling feat of Naresh from the previous day confiscated the rickshaw from the heirless Jumman to present it to Naresh, after touching it up with a quick coat of fresh paint. Naresh was still asleep when the rickshaw was parked in front of the door where he rested. When Naresh finally emerged, still rubbing sleep out of his eyes, one man stretched down to touch his feet. This vegetable farmer was expressing his joy at the arrival of the monsoons so soon after the circus performed by Naresh on the bicycle. Naresh promptly mounted both his feet on the topmost part of the rickshaw, refusing to be worshipped. What he did not refuse was the rickshaw, which he seemed happy to pedal away into the sunset, subdued this day by intimidating clouds.

Over the years, Naresh cultivated an exclusive group of loyal and tested passengers who made sure that he earned enough money to keep the rickshaw well-oiled. The loyalty of his clients rested on his reputation for wanting payment on being served and on never being involved in an accident on the road.

Who was Naresh before he came into our lives? I am told that the mother of Naresh was a large, energetic teenager called Saagiran, from a family of professional toilers in the countryside. My grandmother knew her from the village of the rural side of her family. Like her elders, Saagiran too did odd jobs in my maternal grandmother's palatial ancestral home. Once, she found the courage to confide to my grandmother that she found life in the village too monotonous. My grandmother was already married into a family settled in the city.

"The horizon, the sky, the night and the day look the same every day. The stories you tell me about your life in the city sound so different. I find it difficult to breathe here in so much of nothingness. Take me with you. And I will massage your feet on demand with an oil extracted from an animal now extinct," Saagiran had whispered fiercely to my grandmother after making sure that daylight was finally tamed by nightfall's bewitching darkness.

Saagiran was allowed to accompany my grandmother to the city the following morning, only because she was so plain looking and such a willing worker with a reputation for being a wonder both at broiling as well as sweeping. But once in the city, nothing could get Saagiran to stay indoors and to engage in the chores she was expected to perform. She was mesmerised by the street and stood all day long by the gate wondering where and why the people in different vehicles kept coming and going without pause all day long.

One day a rickshaw stood before her and the driver waited till she made up her mind to step into it. Once Saagiran was seated in the passenger seat, the rickshaw took off and was soon lost in the traffic jam that clogged every corner of the city. My grandmother said that she did worry for a while over Saagiran's sudden disappearance, but she did not do much to really look for her. After a year a stranger knocked on the family door and apologised for having stolen Saagiran from the family. In return he left a bundle at my grandmother's feet and then vanished. When my grandmother looked in-between the sheet of cloth wriggling at her feet she found a baby boy wrapped within the folds, with a tag around his wrist on which it was written "Naresh", or "a king among men". My grandmother had children of different ages of her own so she tried to get Bano Bua to help out. But Bano Bua took such intense dislike to the baby with the Hindu name that my grandmother feared for his life and sent him into hiding to the servants' quarters, where Naresh flowered in the more conducive company of the gardener and the gatekeeper.

WHO DOES BANO BUA THINK SHE IS?

It was not fair on her part to resent Naresh, as Bano Bua came to be with the family almost under similar circumstances. But she made a big fuss over her devout Muslim self and the conflict she faced having to feed and clean a Hindu baby.

"Not possible," she told my grandmother, without fear of the wrath of the grand old lady. But religion could not be the only reason for Bano Bua to refuse to take care of baby Naresh. After all, she was fond of Choti and Moti, the twin daughters of Chabeli, the Dalit who cleaned lavatories in the neighbourhood. But there is no point in asking Bano Bua to explain herself, as talking logic to her is like trying to honk away a cow parked in the middle of a main street in Lucknow. I really don't understand why she is so rude to Naresh, but happy to pamper Choti and Moti with constant hugs and gifts. Since I know there is no way of finding out why Bano Bua does so much the way she does, it is best to avoid talking to her about certain things.

Let me recall for you instead how Bano Bua came to live with my family.

My grandmother was out shopping one day. She was enchanted by the exuberant colours of the vermilion powder piled up in little pyramids on sheets and sheets of sackcloth on the pavement in the Chowk bazaar. My grandmother was Muslim and, unlike married Hindu women, she did not highlight the parting in her hair with vermilion powder. Sometimes she liked to do so, especially when she felt that her husband was too preoccupied to notice her presence. She kept more than a pinch of the powder in the same silver jar that is now in my possession.

"I had turned away from the window to talk to the driver in front. I reminded the driver to return to this street after my visit to the jeweller. I wanted to pick up a kilo of sindoor, along with a hundred glass bangles in red and gold, as gifts for all the women who worked for me in the house. When I straightened myself to address the driver, I saw a twitching black bag sprawled half over the seat and half in-between the space where we put our feet to my right. I screamed and the driver stopped the car with a screech, ripping apart the lace curtain pulled in-between the driver's seat and the passenger's. When the driver looked back I found myself dealing with the shock of seeing his face for the first time in my life, that too so close to my own. I pointed to the big, black mound of movement beside me and he swung to his right to open the door on his side of the car."

This was our favourite bedtime story, told to us ever since I can remember by a grandmother who spiced up the tale with added drama, even where I suspect there was none. Her voice modulated and her eyes opened wide one minute and squeezed into slants in the next as we held our breath and stared at Bano Bua sitting on a low stool beside the bed, her face hidden behind a shawl. Every time the story was told she giggled self-consciously.

Before the driver could open the door of the car, a face had torn itself out of the black robe, begging my grandmother not to throw the creature out of the vehicle.

"They are looking for me. They will take me away and kill me if they find me here," cried the stranger, her delicate face streaked in black from the kajal that streamed down her hollow cheeks from large, almond-brown eyes drowned in terror.

"Take me with you. I will massage your feet at will with oil from an animal now extinct," said the face out of the black robe, and two slender hands grabbed the grandmother's ankles so hard that it hurt.

For a split second my grandmother wondered where she had heard that line before, but realising the urgency of the situation she decided to debate all doubts that crossed her mind later. She ordered the driver to race the car as fast as he could out of Chowk. He hesitated, but of course he dared not to disobey.

At that time Bano Bua was not yet 20 years old. She was being forced into a marriage with the 55-year-old husband of her older sister, who was sold away to a brothel in Chowk because she had given birth to a third girl. Her daughters were also bought by the same pimp, along with her. A wedding was planned between the elderly gentleman-without-shame and Bano Bua, in the hope that she would give birth to the son he longed for. Maybe the "son and not daughter" thing was not even an issue in the mind of this gentleman, but just an excuse to hide his desire to touch and feel the body of younger and different women every now and then. The man's first marriage was at the age of 25, and his back had already been turned on two other wives before Bano Bua's sister.

The older sister wanted to help a miserable Bano Bua out of this preposterous proposal, but there seemed no way out. Bano Bua had sneaked out of her house to visit her sister in Chowk. The sister said that she was much happier at the brothel, far away from her parents, who proved to be hopelessly unhelpful, and a husband who was indifferent. For the first time in her life she had an earning of her own and liked living in the company of so many other working women. She invited Bano Bua to stay with her at the brothel. But Bano Bua was not comfortable with that option. She embraced her sister, thanked her for her hospitality and got back into the burqa, the overgarment in black that made her anonymous on the street. The burqa had proven to be a great prop at this hour, when she did not want to attract attention to herself, as she took to the stairs of the brothel to visit her sister, and now as she climbed down in search of a future.

The burqa helped to hide her individuality and made it easy for her to get lost in the crowd on the notorious street. But as she walked on she had little clue as to what to do next. This is before she spied my grandmother, smiling to herself behind the glass window of her car. Bano Bua used the window-rattling din of the marketplace and the confusion caused by the traffic jam that day to imagine my grandmother's smile as an invitation to sit beside her in the car. Desperation to save her life had made Bano Bua exceptionally bold and she opened the door of the car to sneak in. Of course my grandmother took Bano Bua under her custody and taught her the lesson of a lifetime to never allow anyone to threaten her dignity.

Bano Bua was 25 years old when I was born. For many years after their marriage, my parents had no children. The paternal grandmother was the proud mother of five sons, my father being the youngest and, unfortunately for my mother, the most pampered child. My father's mother had a peculiar way of exhibiting her love for her son, mainly by looking down upon his wife and constantly taunting them both as a couple for not having children. My mother probably froze in fright at the thought of conceiving a child that may not be a boy. We don't know. We will never know. For soon after I was born, she died, probably too petrified even to find out what she had given birth to. That is how I came to grow up in the home of my maternal grandmother. Bano Bua, brimming with much confidence by that time, just took it upon herself to lord over my life, which she continues to do to this day.

That is how Bano Bua got to befriend Dr Meena Singh. The topic of Meena's research was the case of the courtesans of Lucknow. Family friends, who were aware of Bano Bua's background, told Meena about us. Bano Bua had not seen her sister for many years. She was tired of sneaking in and out of the red-light area and in the lanes of Chowk as if she were a criminal. So she put an end to the visits. And it was too complicated for Bano Bua's sister to visit us. Even so, my grandmother had smuggled the sister from Chowk into the house one season on the festive occasion of *Idul Fitr,* the most important feast that follows after the last day of a month of fasting by Muslims around the world. She did this perhaps to quench her own curiosity about a courtesan, who enjoyed the reputation among nobility of being the "other" and "the sinful woman". My grandmother had probably never seen a courtesan in flesh and blood and this was her first and last chance to do so. Amidst the confusion of the crowds that constantly streamed into the house on the auspicious day, none of the others noticed the courtesan from Chowk. Not even the menfolk, as the sister sat silently in one corner of Bano Bua's room, munching on betel leaves that dyed her mouth a red deeper than the colour of blood.

It was only my grandmother who stared that day to her heart's content at Bano Bua's sister. She tried to find in her what she had read Leopold von Orlich, a German traveller, say about the Lucknow courtesan when he visited Chowk in the mid-19th century:

> They were all bare headed and their beautiful black hair fell down in braids or was interwoven with jewels. Most of them wore large nose rings which hung over the corners of the mouth and their large ear rings touched their shoulders. Very few of them could be called pretty but they have piercing eyes which look the more brilliant because their eye lids are blackened with antimony a coloured scarf was thrown lightly and gracefully over the neck and shoulders and displayed rather than concealed the fine contour of the upper part of their persons they did not fail to make many remarks upon us and sought to draw our attention by laughing, joking and tittering but it is by no means advisable to pay any attention to them, as these bayderes are extremely importunate.

Now Bano Bua was over the moon at the thought of visiting her sister after such a long time and in the august company of a research scholar. She bounced about like a queen bee as she waited to be chauffeured to Chowk without a burqa. She waited to embrace her sister once again and to introduce Dr Meena Singh to her.

MY GRANDMOTHER

When my grandmother was a young woman in Lucknow, it was not possible for her to slip into shoes and just walk out of the front door whenever she felt like it. Those were the days when it was a lot easier for the aristocratic patriarch to preserve his vanity by inventing rules and regulations that he said were in the best interest of the whole family. While he did not trust his women on the street, he had allowed himself the freedom to float in and out of the arms of the wife or wives at home and the courtesan in her first-floor chambers in Chowk. The women then had little choice except to flutter around the four walls of the home similar to the fate of a bird in a cage. The lifelong confinement imposed upon women made poets of some of the more imaginative ones, like the anonymous one who scribbled:

> My captor! Give me leave to at least flap my wings
> This is my very first day in your cage.

There was the courtesan Janaki Bai Chapanchuri in the 1920s, whose singing was sweeter than a nightingale's and whose spectacular dance performances were self-taught. The entire city was in love with her, but there was one man who wanted to also possess her, patronise her and buy her. When he was told that Janaki Bai was not for sale, the pompous man with pockets full of money felt insulted and in a fit of rage grabbed a knife to stab the one he claimed to love 56 times. The tragic incident immortalised the woman Janaki Bai Chapanchuri. From a rich collection of poems left by Janaki Bai of 56 Knives, my favourite lines are:

> To this day my heart's lament has not touched my lips,
> My wailing remains the secret of one who is veiled.

When in need of anything outside the four walls of the home, ladies from aristocratic families, like my grandmother, were expected to simply send a message to the cloth merchant, to the jeweller or to the doctor, and the wares and the expertise were delivered to the doorstep. The groceries were deposited to the kitchen in the same way. Since times constantly change, my grandmother was eventually given permission to go shopping once in a while to the bazaar. But the thought of the way it was done makes me giggle today.

The patriarch was first informed. After permission was granted, the driver needed time to pave the path from the front door of the house to the back door of the automobile with a screen with the help of minions lesser than himself. My grandmother did not wear a burqa, which many Muslim women are expected to wear even today. She had dressed in flowing skirts made from six yards of satin or taffeta cloth. The top was always full-sleeved and reached down to her thigh in a material that matched the billowing gharara, worn from the waist down to the feet. Another three yards of chiffon were wrapped like a shawl over the outfit and also covered the head.

Women were expected to plaster themselves with a cake of modesty that often wiped out much of their real self. Wrists were wrapped in bracelets, the neck negated by chains and chokers, earlobes lay hidden behind jewels on hooks and rings, and the nose was lost to sparkling studs. Decorated with so many riches, they looked wonderful, but it also slowed women down, especially when they were in a hurry to get on with life. Dressed in this way, my grandmother would almost tiptoe out of the house, keeping close to the canvas screens, her head slightly lowered, to slide into the back seat of the car, which was curtained off with lots of frills from the driver in front. The belief was that women from respectable homes should be neither seen nor heard by the rest of the world whether they were in pain or pleasure. Don't ask me why.

The Austin from the 1950s would navigate its way in great dignity alongside pedestrians, cyclists, rickshaws, horse carts, carriages, and cows either sitting or standing in the middle of the road. Chowk, the oldest crossroads in the city, is where merchants have been meeting with madams, and scholars with scoundrels, since times lost to memory. Once in the middle of the marketplace, my grandmother would clear the curtain away from the glass window a little in greedy desperation to find out what the world was up to. From this safe distance of her hiding place, she allowed herself the freedom to look at the world without allowing the world to see her.

Once the car slowed down to a snail's pace in the crowded belly of the street of the silversmith, she shamelessly stared at shopkeepers, sitting with their legs crossed on the floor, a turban wrapped around the head, their cream-coloured shirts in silk patched with sweat marks under the arms, around the stomach and back. A red dot was always smeared on the forehead if they were Hindu, while Muslim artisans and merchants wore skullcaps and dressed in long shirts and loose pyjamas in cotton cloth that was starched crisp and was always the colour of snow. The shops were little cubicles all in a row on the right and left of the narrow street, selling hand-hammered jewellery in filigree in one enclosure and cluttered with more gold and silver in another. Beaten brassware had beckoned from one booth. The egg-yolk yellows, leaf greens and chilli reds displayed in the many flower shops were described by my grandmother as endless paint oozing out of different-coloured tubes. When she spied a lone group of palanquin bearers swinging their way through the crowded lanes of the busy marketplace, she could not help but recall a poem from the days when political activists were also poets. My grandmother recited what Indira Solomon, her English teacher, had taught her about Sarojini Naidu, famously called the Nightingale of India. Sarojini Naidu was the first female president of the Indian National Congress, and the first governor of Uttar Pradesh in post-independent India till 1949. One of the poems she wrote while in Lucknow is the song of the palanquin bearer.

> Lightly, O lightly we bear her along,
> She sways like a flower in the wind of our song;
> She skims like a bird on the foam of a stream,
> She floats like a laugh from the lips of a dream.
> Gaily, O gaily we glide and we sing,
> We bear her along like a pearl on a string.

> Softly, O softly we bear her along,
> She hangs like a star in the dew of our song;
> She springs like a beam on the brow of the tide,
> She falls like a tear from the eyes of a bride.
> Lightly, O lightly we glide and we sing,
> We bear her along like a pearl on a string.

When she saw foodstuff being fired in another shop, she just had to defy the family tradition and roll the window just that little bit lower so that she could inhale the forbidden aromas of jalebis, samosas and *imartis* to her heart's delight. It required even greater courage on her part to paste herself closer to the flat glass and to raise that sly gaze above the shops in search of women, often in and out of wooden balconies carved in patterns that vied with the delicate designs found on the gold and silver jewellery sold below. The balconies were quite empty during the day but some female voices could be heard rehearsing their music, and the sound of many anklets added to the enigmatic life lived on the first floor of this marketplace.

Sometimes an entire song would escape through bamboo curtains for the world to hear.

> Tell the lovers here to hold their tears before we meet,
> Otherwise the road to your house will be closed if there is
> flooding in the street.

These women did not mind being seen. Once in a while they emerged out of the interior of their homes to grace the balconies overlooking the street, with bare midriffs draped often with nothing more than a shawl cut from see-through nylon cloth, smiling down at pedestrians and waving out to others. Families like my grandmother's had called people living above the shops in Chowk women of ill repute, even though many male members from families like my grandmother's were known to enjoy a close, long and more fulfilling relationship with women here than with any other human being in their life. Since respectable women rarely got to meet with the coquettish courtesans, they held a particular fascination for those who were a little devilish at heart, like my grandmother.

There was a wedding in the family and my grandmother wanted to order fresh flowers for the celebrations. She wanted to look at some more jewellery and bring back yards of different kinds of cloth as gifts for the poor, and the wealthy guests expected to participate in the happy occasion. But fate had other plans for her and she was forced to return home that day with none of the things she had hoped to pick up, except Bano Bua.

THE COURTESAN

When in the mood for it, I love to step out of the house and into the city with Bano Bua. She knows the place like the back of her hand and her love for Lucknow is most infectious. To pause with her at any corner here is to inspire her to tell yet another tale about another brick from ancient times, when the city was known as Lakshman Tila, perhaps Lakhan Qila, or even from before. Most interesting to listen to is also the gossip that she brings home about families living on both banks of the Gomti, another river in the country that has forgotten to flow. Then I love to hear her speak when she talks in the traditional language unique to the city, peppering it with vivacious expressions from local dialects in such a charming way that it is my dream to one day try and capture the nuance of many things she says in Urdu in English.

Without knowing a single word of English, Bano Bua has organised my papers into folders with different colours. She is so clever. All my notes on the work of Meena are tucked between the covers of a red folder. In her head she has titled the folder *Kothewali Bibi* or "Lady of the First Floor". The title is in honour of all the steps that Meena has climbed up and down in an attempt to explore and not to exploit the world of the scarlet women of the city.

Today, these women are the city's most neglected citizens. The former courtesans are forced into common prostitution. Some still live on the first floor above shops in Chowk. The latticework on the attractive wooden balconies is now rotten, and its many parts are even seen hanging by a nail, as if unable to bear the weight of the legendary hospitality displayed by these magnanimous women in the past.

I have known of Meena from much before her work with the beauties of the bazaar. It goes back to La Martiniere Girls' School, where my teacher in kindergarten was called Miss Rosebottom. From kindergarten till I finished school, I was always one of the tallest students in class. This could be one reason why my appetite was so voracious. When I lived on the school premises as a boarder, I had always felt more famished than a fakir. I made it a habit in the dining hall, which was more imposing than the menu it served, to receive food into my plate from the portion of other fusspot students who missed home-cooked meals. They would pass me a good part from their lunch and dinner when the teacher was not looking, as we sat in the school dining hall with folded hands and eyes closed to thank the Lord for what we were about to receive. I was always left feeling hungry after what we received at each meal of lamb curry and rice at lunch, and stewed meat at dinner with only two pieces of chapatti, which I would have liked to have a few more of. The school served me food in miserably small portions, I thought, leaving me to always feel hungry. That is why, after every midday meal, I would head for the corridor below Khurshid Manzil, the 19th-century building of the school. Khurshid Manzil, or "The House of the Sun", was built in imitation of Windsor Castle by the ruler Saadat Ali Khan for his favourite wife Khurshidzadi. Here I would stand at a dignified distance, deeply breathing the aroma of food freshly cooked, brought to school by servants in several-tiered tiffin carriers for the day scholars. The fragrance that I liked best was also the one that made my stomach ache the most for more food.

I could do little more than to longingly look at the corner where Meena sat on one side of a long wooden bench with a row of siblings and cousins. I saw her from the back as she lunched away on a meal laid out on cemented tables extending out of the wall. I did not belong to the same gang of friends as Meena's younger sister, who was in my class. But every so often I chatted her up in the hope that she would bring me some more cheese and tomato sandwiches from the hotel kitchen owned by her parents. Since the boarders were strictly forbidden to eat food brought from outside the school, we would rudely grab the box of sandwiches, made of thin white cardboard, and disappear into that part of the premises where the toilets stood in a row. Locked inside one of the toilets—away from the gaze of the matron on duty, who always looked for an opportunity to cane us—Joan Yeoward and I would gobble up the sandwiches after having hastily snapped open the strings tied around the box. Joan was my best friend and the swiftest athlete of our times. She had also mastered the technique of clasping the cane of matrons, teachers and the principal in mid-air before it could crack down on her palm.

Meena's lunch had to be the best in town; after all, it came from the kitchen of the Carlton Hotel, owned by her family. This was the oldest hotel in town, built by an Englishman who was inconsolable at being so far away from his favourite Carlton in London.

Over the years, a certain style was born of the way meals were best enjoyed at the Lucknow Carlton. When we were told that we could join the elders at the hotel for a meal, the announcement was treated with great awe. The children were excited at the thought of another visit to the sprawling and meticulously manicured lawns of the Carlton Hotel, where it was possible to play at a safe distance from the grown-ups without disturbing their chit-chatting. The joy was in waiting for delicacies that came from the kitchen inside. Under a canopy in one corner of the garden, *kakori* kebabs had simmered at their own pace on gigantic plates placed over a fire of coals. As I grew older I noticed how Meena's family from the Punjab was different from the Punjabi refugees who came to Lucknow after the country was divided to create Pakistan in 1947. Most upper-crust Muslims left landlocked Lucknow for an alien city by the sea in Pakistan, in anticipation of a more prosperous life among strangers who were also Muslim. Lucknow had accommodated thousands of Hindu refugees, mostly petty shopkeepers from the markets in Lahore, who were settled in the large open space of the park built in the Aminabad area in 1911. The refugees lost no time in getting on with business and with life. They parked their wares on packing cases turned upside down and started to buy and sell, giving that part of Aminabad its second name of Refugee Market. Aminabad was populated by Aminudaullah, a learned minister of Amjad Ali Shah, fourth king of Avadh.

Meena's family came to Avadh before the 1947 partition to do business and to one day buy the palatial Carlton Hotel from its British owners. The private life of the family was screened away from the street by the leafy landscape of the Carlton Hotel gardens, with hedges that were trimmed higher than some of the oldest trees. The pace of its household seemed as leisurely as that of the former rulers of Avadh. Above all the family combined its commercial pursuits with a love for learning. Bano Bua pointed out that when these people spoke, it did not feel like bullets hailing down a tin roof. This family was proof that Punjabis, when they live in Lucknow, no longer remain Punjabi like Punjabis elsewhere in the world. Like all the different people who have made Lucknow their home, certain Avadhi ways creep into their life as well, like speaking with a lilt and behaving less boisterously.

The Punjab, the land of five rivers, is a fascinating territory as well. It is one of the gateways into South Asia. For thousands of years, people have criss-crossed the Punjab on their way out of South Asia or on a visit to this part of the world. There is a written record of Alexander's coming here, some 300 years before the birth of Christ. Alexander spent a month in northwest South Asia, mainly nursing his many battle wounds. Soon after he died, Chandragupta Maurya conquered the land from Seleucus, the Macedonian general of Alexander and his successor in South Asia. Bano Bua believes that the Mauryan dynasty gets its name from Mora, Chandragupta's mother. She thinks it was extremely clever of the founder of the Mauryan dynasty to marry the daughter of Seleucus to make peace instead of more war with the Greeks. That good idea went on to boost trade with the Hellenistic world, encouraging a hectic citizen-to-citizen contact with all the worlds that existed beyond the Indian subcontinent. The Mauryans had ruled one of the largest and most magnificent empires in the world, from Bengal to the Hindu Kush, and the people then had basked in unimaginable multiculturalism millennia before the phrase was coined by social scientists in modern times. Back then the different views of the world according to Buddhism, Hinduism, Hellenism and Zoroastrianism were expressed without fear, and with heads held high.

The region of Gandhara in northwest South Asia is connected to Ayodhya as it was the domain of Bharat, a brother of Ram. Taxila and Peshawar in the Gandhara territory got their names after the sons of Bharat. And Gandhari, the queen of the blind king Dhritarashtra from the *Mahabharata,* is from this region. The kingdom was probably named after *gandha,* the aroma of flowers found here in abundance along with fauna and a lush growth of herbs that bewitch people to this day.

The place was ruled by several Indo-Greek dynasties before a horde of tribes, mainly from Central Asia, some a mixture of Turco-Iranian people, came to make a home here. There were the Scythians, Bactrians, Parthians and Huns, all of whom have surely contributed to giving Indians like Meena and most of her family members a fair complexion.

Muslim warriors came to South Asia much, much later, Bano Bua argues with all those who insist that it is Islam that introduced war and conflict among the peace-loving and non-violent populations of ancient South Asia.

"How do *you* know, you illiterate woman?" she was once questioned by a visitor in an unusually mean tone of voice.

"From the company of educated people I keep," Bano Bua would bark back at all those who tried to insult her and to question her knowledge about the ways of the world.

Zoroastrian ideas had fascinated the Kushans, and the founder of this dynasty was Chinese. The greatest of all Kushans was Kanishka from the 2nd century, who patronised Buddhism and is buried in his capital city of Purusapura, now Peshawar in modern-day Pakistan. Although it is uncertain what language Kanishka spoke, inscriptions in Greek were found from his time as the ruler of a huge empire. His kingdom stretched from the Xinjiang province in modern northwest China, over Afghanistan, northwest Pakistan, Ayodhya and Patna.

Rulers like Kanishka were interested in all the different views of the world, making Taxila cosmopolitan. By the time Muhammad, the messenger of Islam, died in 632 AD, Gandhara was a civilisation brought to its knees by the marauding tribe of the white Huns, who were more attracted to Hinduism and less to Buddhism.

The family of Meena may even resemble the first Turkic warriors, seen for the first time in Lucknow around the 11th century, who had probably stayed back in the Indo-Gangetic plains from the army of Mahmud of Ghazni. A warrior of Turkic origin, Ghazni had thundered down inhospitable Himalayan mountains out of hunger for minerals found in such plenty on the vast alluvial fields encircling Lucknow. He did not make a home in the Indian subcontinent but returned after each attack to Ghazni, his capital city in the barren mountains of modern-day Afghanistan, to enjoy the fruits of his loot of India.

The women in Meena's family are nearly as tall as the men, each one of them with a straight back, slender limbs, light skin of the molten gold kind, thick black eyebrows and dark hair that swings far below the waistline. Just imagine the wealth of experience and familiarity with a treasure of unfamiliar ideas that migrants like them must have brought to life in the landlocked region of Avadh.

Now I wait for the dust that collects around us during the course of each day during this season to be cleared by Bano Bua before asking her to look for a folder of essays for me. The essays give me an interesting twist to every shibboleth that most of us accept as God's own truth. Do not blame dowry, an essay says in one place, referring to the social custom despised today for being responsible for the murder of many women in several parts of India. According to Meena, dowry constituted voluntary gifts given by the bride's parents, kin and sometimes the whole village at the time of marriage, but under British rule a masculine economy took shape. This diminished the woman's control over her own life and over the system in which she lived. British laws are blamed for bringing an economic upheaval upon what was till then a safety net for women.

"Bua, where is the paper I planned to read after dinner?" I slammed a book on the table and dropped a pen or two that rolled noisily on the floor. Like a spoilt child, I continued to search for the case of the courtesan.

"Which one?" she called back, popping out of the kitchen with a cup of *yakhni,* the chicken broth cooked in aromatic herbs that heals the soul. "There is no need for you to blow like a horn, Bibi. All that you have are papers. May I know exactly what paper you are looking for? And do allow me a minute to find it for you," Bano Bua said, converting a cute cut-out from an outdated calendar into a coaster. She put it on the table before me and placed a piping-hot cup of soup upon it.

The brew smelt divine but I was laughing at the delightful word Bano Bua had used in Urdu to chide me for my childish tantrum. She had just accused me of being as noisy and as useless as a *bhopoo,* a kind of horn. Then watching me wordless with amusement she compared me to the capricious climate in places far away, where she had heard it was warm one minute and cold in the next.

"Remember not to spill any of the brew. The spell will weaken with each drop wasted. Now what is it that you can't find? Do you mean the paper in the red cover? The one written by the Kothewali Bibi?"

On my nodding a yes she went to look for it.

I reached out for the drink, still chuckling to myself, without forgetting that it was no ordinary soup that I held.

At dinner, earlier in the evening, I was warned that I would receive the soup, sanctified with a set of special prayers. Bano Bua will brew the same soup for anyone feeling under the weather. The prayers that garnish the brew are always different, depending on the problem of the person, who is expected to drink it. In my case, Bano Bua was hoping that I would find a groom if I sipped the drink in the correct manner after dinner.

We eat dinner early by Lucknow standards. It is often sliced cucumbers sprinkled with salt and crushed black pepper, and yoghurt with roasted cumin seeds whipped into it. Chicken is cooked only once in a while. The dough for the round, flat bread baked translucent is kneaded from whole-wheat flour and prepared on a tawa, a cast iron plate. This bread we eat with kofta, which in Turkish means meatballs. Since we have considerably modified the mouth watering mutton-and-grease-based meals served in many other homes in Lucknow, our kofta is made not from minced meat but grated pumpkin. Many homes here still serve four meals a day throughout the year, including a combination of non-vegetarian but almost vegetable-less dishes, accompanied by rice, bread, and a slice of halwa or spoon of kheer, made more delicious with added sugar, nuts and milk, cooked dry into *khoya.* A siesta after the midday meal is invariably followed by snacks at teatime like samosas or pakoras, and often the last meal is enjoyed after midnight. The above menu, however, is no match to what the aristocracy had served in the city only a century ago, and before. At that time, a contest between trained quails on the dining table had flagged off many a royal banquet. The birds had to first win a hotly contested pecking match. The winners of several such rounds were loudly lauded, of course. They were then carried ceremoniously by minions in uniforms into the kitchen to be dressed in an exotic batter of flour and egg whites whipped into a flood of froth, and deep-fried. But the timing of the royal chefs was so subtle that the delicacy did not linger in the fire a second longer than was necessary. Once brought to the table, the crisp coating cracked like the shell of a freshly laid egg on the guest's plate and the quail popped out, free to fly away once again.

This wondrous act was followed by the sudden entry of 49 maidens, divided into seven groups of seven dancers, each group dressed in the seven colours of the rainbow to salute the host for having provided such a spectacle.

Bano Bua and I do not live like that. We cannot afford to live like that. Besides, the naturally intelligent Bano Bua realises that moderation is key to a healthy way of life. Over the years she has taught me to savour the bitter gourd more than biryani, lentils more than lamb, and cucumbers more than kebabs, especially when they are freshly plucked from nearby farms.

Watching me wide awake hours after we have finished dinner and finding me staring into space, Bano Bua wants to know if I am unable to make up my mind whether to read or to write in that hour. My reply is a silent smile. Her hand goes to her back to look for that end of her sari where she twists coins into a knot for use during an emergency. She brings the corner from under one arm before pulling out a coin from the knot.

"Head or tail?"

"Head," I giggle.

And when Bano Bua tosses the coin it does fall on its head, signalling to me to choose reading over writing. I take the folder in my hand, but before I can open it the ceiling fan whirrs to a gradual standstill as the electricity vanishes unexpectedly.

I hear Bano Bua swear into nothingness, as if we have been thrown into the dark for the first time in our lives. This happens all year round in Lucknow, in heat and in cold, at daytime and at night, and never with a warning. And each time that the electricity disappears, Bano Bua swears with the same intensity as the last time we had experienced similar agony. Then there is silence.

"No, Bua, I don't need a candle," I insist, not wanting to say or hear much more as I begin to enjoy the darkness around me. I am determined not to allow a temperature of 40 degrees Celsius to daunt me. Despite the "no", I spy a tiny flame floating as if by itself towards the pool of darkness that I had wanted to drown myself in. I watch the flame lower itself down to a spot not too far away from where I sit. My empty cup is mysteriously refilled with some more soup, spreading the fragrances I like so much.

I bring the cup of soup as close as possible to my face to feast on whiff after whiff of the heady aroma from the garam masala one minute, and of onion and garlic the next. I test the temperature of the soup with a finger and fish out a juicy chunk of ginger that surfaces in a coat of some coriander leaves. As I chew on the ginger root, enjoying its tang, I thank the Lord for the cup before me so full.

Soft cloth dipped surely in rose water comes to caress the limbs and to wash away all the swelter of a balmy summer evening, while a handheld fan, waving unseen in the semi-darkness, tries to keep me cool.

Then I wait for her conversation to trail away. When the electricity went, it carried with it much of Bano Bua's talk with someone across the hedge in the garden, leaving me alone in the dark. I snuggle a little closer to the window and notice how nothing else is visible anymore between myself and the Gomti, which waits for the monsoons to make it swell up like a mother-to-be.

I find her looking at me staring at her. And she stirs. Then I see her rise out of her depth. She stretches up, wearing all the sins of man, somewhat breathless from want of oxygen but still smiling, her face painted mud-gold with muck and mucus.

As she floats nearer I see pieces of empty liquor and milk containers pinned to her flowing tresses. The tunic that trails behind her drips with poison from acts of wasteful industrial and religious rituals that continue to billow pollution into her waters in deadly proportions.

Mysteriously, I am able to step out of the four walls I sat in and go out to meet her halfway in the darkness. Once we are face-to-face I see some of the riddles of the world revealed in her eyes. I wonder what it is that she sees in mine.

A wave unfolds and a fistful of stars are dropped at my feet. I respond by trying to hold the river in an embrace. She smells of all the rubbish released into the river by factory owners.

Once again I try to cradle her and carry her to the stainless steel shower in my bathroom for a good scrub. The people along its banks will just have to wait for the river to return. What else can I do to protect the Gomti from over three million people who pump their excrement into her waters through dozens of drains, and to prevent the city from taking her goodness for granted? I want to ask them all if they have forgotten why the river is sacred. Do they wait for the river to dry up before they realise the worth of water, or what?

On the way I exhale smoke still clinging to what I imagine is the lap of the river. I swim towards my home, further away from the call of bells from the many temples on the shore. The musing of muezzins from masjids grows faint, and so does the animated conversation of the *chataka* birds glued to tree tops in wait to welcome the first cloud.

I feel I have placed the river on the hard floor of my bathroom and below the shower. I twist the knob to rain down water upon the river. I lather a herbal shampoo into her foul-smelling hair, braided with dead weeds and plastic bags and pick away pieces of all kinds of other mechanical, animal and human waste collected in the crevices of the river over centuries. With a cake of sandal soap I rub the sinuousness before me and while she is being rinsed I discover that she has the sun hidden deep inside her navel.

When she begins to sparkle a little I mop the daughter of Ganga as gently as I can. I notice how much she resembles her mother at that hour. She looks as fresh as the Ganga at the glacier-covered mountain of Gangotri.

Then she is still as sleep, her breathing so transparent that the sulphuric depth of her basin is laid bare for the world to see. This is how I imagine she must have first revealed herself in prehistoric times to Rama. This is how she must have looked with her green gait flanked by blue shores.

After the scrub and the nap she is ready for a date on a day when swallows sing. The river shifts as swans and cranes crowd its shores. I plunge into the water.

I want Bano Bua to go away and leave me to fantasise over music from European bands playing on the riverbank and ending in a thunderous encore. I want to sit here and imagine the last spark from the fabulous fireworks dim at its own pace.

With several sighs of regret I bid farewell to the steam engine freshly arrived from Birmingham to increase the supply of water in the Gomti. There is the royal barge fitted with the head of a swan designed by Robert Home, the court artist till 1828. I wave to the boat painted green, fitted with the head of a peacock at one end, and towed by an elephant to the punt, till both drift out of mind. I feast my eyes for the last time on ballerinas balanced on the gilded tail of another boat. I spot the boat named Sultan of Avadh. There is the great schooner with three masts, its partitions tailored from velvet, the teak floor covered in Persian rugs and seats decked in gold brocade, now swiftly sailing away from memory. I must remain on deck till the candle making its round to each *shair* reaches the prince among poets, who is always the last to recite his verse at the night-long mushaira held on boats shaped like fishes. I must not forget to request an encore from each of Lucknow's literati present.

And there it is, the lovely last strain from the *rubaiyat* of Raghupati Sahai Firaq Gorakhpuri, who died in 1982 but wrote in the luscious style of the 11th-century Persian poet Omar Khayyam.

> When stars did dazzle so bold,
> When dew was dropped from heaven's gold,
> Inspired by silence and then urged by grace
> With a touch of silk she parted her fold.

The river sweeps me to the scattered remains of what was once an impressive walled city on the Lakshman Tila. This is perhaps the home of the first Muslim settlers. Over time Lucknow's fame as the private domain of powerful Sheikh and Pathan clans spread across the seven seas. The inner city on the Lakshman Tila was fortified with a thick wall of defence. From the parapet of the high fort, a close eye was kept on all the boats sailing up and down the river, laden with luxury goods from around the world. It is from here that local boats were flagged off carrying back equally precious parcels of indigo, muslin, sugar and spices.

I look up at the hillock, but all that I see now is the administrative block of the present-day medical college raised on the ruins of the medieval city. There is a row of a few other buildings left over from the past that have turned their backs on the water today. Watching my face fall, the river lifts it up with a cool splash and twirls itself around me one step at a time at first. And then it goes ballistic till the present fades away once more.

I am drowned in the memory of musicians, standing on the outer portal of the Machchi Bhawan on the Tila to announce each dawn and dusk on the *shehnai.* Many more images emerge as the river gradually brings its flash performance to a finish.

In the late 18th century, when Asafudaulah ruled from Lucknow, he did not move into the Machchi Bhawan complex but built Daulat Khana for himself. The Rumi Darwaza came up in the same neighbourhood near the impressive Bada Imambara. About a century later after the first war of independence in 1857, the needs of the British, the new masters of the city, had changed. The British wanted the city to be safe, orderly, clean, and loyal, and to pay for all these facilities. From an imperial capital, Lucknow was groomed into a typical colonial city where life revolved around the cantonment and military operations. The lives of civilians in the Chowk area was ignored in the hope that the artisans, gardeners and cooks would perish out of neglect. The rhythmic sound of hammers of workers beating sheets of silver into wafer-thin slivers dimmed. The fragrance from shops selling perfumes, scented oil and incense mingled with fumes from open drains. Sweetmeats were covered under a thick blanket of flies, and flower vendors wept to watch their plants wilt.

All the frills and lace embroidered once in gold thread was replaced by rayon and synthetic and even more plastic and is passed off today as silk, satin and brocade.

The Machchi Bhawan takes its time to appear. The waves are still uneven. I wait for the water to calm down before craning the neck to watch the fort take form. A rub of the eyes enables the vision of the five palaces of the Panch Mahal. It is shimmering glory, its walls emblazoned with millions of fish motifs with a finish in silver. There is the naked sword, placed in the centre of the lofty arcade of the portal, decorated with 52 fishes. A notice warns visitors to lower the head before entering the palace, and to those who have come uninvited to face the sword dangling above them at their own risk. At that time, whoever ruled the Machchi Bhawan ruled Lucknow.

Now the river has me perched at the exact spot where Thomas Daniell had moored his boat and made a memorable sketch of the Machchi Bhawan in 1789. Along with William, his painter nephew, Thomas came to Lucknow in a bullock cart. The two English artists had walked part of the way from Kolkata, and some of the journey was covered in a palanquin. They had abandoned home and hearth in Europe to seek romance. To finance their lust for wandering, they looked for patrons to pay them for immortalising on canvas the thrill that the British said they had found in the landscape here.

A flood of European artists and later photographers followed to capture the courtly leisure and wonder of this place. In the archives, there is a 1772 portrait of ruler Shujaudaula by Tilly Kettle, one of the first English painters to look for princely patrons in India. Kettle's realistic style influenced local artists.

French painter Antoine-Louis Henri de Polier loved to wear a turban and local garb. He learnt to sit on the floor and, supported by cushions behind him, he was mesmerised watching dancers perform in the verandah. Polier lived in India for 30 years and amassed a huge amount of money. He was the owner of rare manuscripts and paintings, which he took back with him to France. There were other painters who marvelled at the river's tireless caressing of the buildings standing at its shore and have captured this on canvas. Ozias Humphry, the English portrait painter, worked here in 1785, before he went blind in 1792; artists William Hodges and Robert Home have enjoyed painting in Lucknow when a lot of commuting was done by boat.

With the loss in power of the Sheikhs and Pathans and the rise of the Nawabs of Avadh in the 18th century, the Pancha Mahal and the Machchi Bhawan were made to share walls with the Daulat Khana, the residence that Asafudaulah built for himself. Asafudaulah's close friend Claude Martin built his home nearby on two levels, into the river. He called it the Farhat Baksh Kothi.

In the early 19th century the Chattar Manzil was built. This was a sprawling palace crowned with *chattri*, or umbrellas in gold-plated stone on the terrace and it had separate suites for bathing and for bedding for women and eunuchs. The Chattar Manzil was once flanked by Moorish minarets and courtyards overflowing with fountains and flowers, which reminded tourists of that time of the garden of delight mentioned in the *Arabian Nights*. With the coming of the automobile, the riverfront entrance of Chattar Manzil was closed. Its main doors opened on the opposite side of the building on a busy street in post-independent India. The former palace of Lucknow's royalty was converted into the main office of the Central Drugs and Research Institute.

Now vacated and empty, the only royal palace to survive in Lucknow waits to be restored into a museum or a cultural centre—or will it be left to disappear into debris?

MORE MYTHS

After the river runs out of stories from around this side of the bank, it carries me to a different mound, piled up tall on many more myths. The folklore here is that once upon a time Lucknow was the way it was meant to be. That is before heaven and Earth separated. When both beginning and end were just a ball of mist suspended in eternal darkness. There was no time. There was just eternity. Reality was dreamlike and infinite.

Then creation emerged out of this whirlpool of nothing to give form to foam. Space yielded under the divine footsteps of eternal existence to leave uneven contours that hardened into mountains and many hills.

Dawn sighed on being shaken out of slumber and air enveloped ether. Day was forced to dissolve into dusk and fire was born to dot the void with a thousand beads of sweat that routinely evaporated into clouds. Brown went to colour Earth and greenery sprouted everywhere. Blue was splashed into the sky and a deeper shade was reserved for the sea. A sprinkle of gold made timber glow and on its crown collected different shades of green. Sheets of flora were spread out below all the greens, and beyond that fauna frolicked. An elderly bark tried to cool a breakaway limb from itself in water that slipped to float far. When the piece of wood chanced upon a mooring it became a boat. Some other splinters of wood bobbed up and down in the water like fish. One out of this playful lot flew so high above the water that it grew wings. Once it learnt all the ways of the birds and the insects, it dropped an egg into the Gomti, the river that is fortunate to have witnessed the first creation on Earth. Out of this splash of the egg into the Gomti, a man, a woman, a boy and a girl soon surfaced.

According to the most playful legend in town, the children of the cosmic egg swam around in glee till they followed the aroma of sandalwood and found a log most comfortable. They used it as a raft and floated on the river for a while. Then they drifted towards the shore. With a little help from the sturdy bamboo bushes on the banks of the river, they finally stepped upon land to become the first family of Lucknow.

It is presumed that humans then were without thought about a superior nation, religion, caste, class or complexion. Nothing except love engaged these people. Naturally, humanity multiplied and prospered. New generations came into being and for a while love, peace and unity made the world go round. Heroic deeds kept humanity in good humour, but conceit, pride, greed, jealousy, wealth and power crept into life to make some people less pleased than others. Then anger ruled. In these terrifying moments, if compassion was able to black out fury, then all was well again. But if disgust conquered and was allowed to call the shots, the consequences led to suffering. Often, to unimaginable human suffering.

In the absence of not much more information of such historic times, it can only be imagined that the cycle of deep affection among humanity continued to alternate with quarrels, like light every day follows darkness, and day gives way to night. That cycle is natural. What is unnatural is for darkness to overstay its welcome and to block all light at the end of the tunnel of life. Not much more was known of the likes and dislikes of those people for many millennia till the story of Ayodhya was told to us by Valmiki.

From the epic *Ramayana* we know that Rama had ruled Ayodhya. He was born some 8,000 years ago in the lunar month of March, when the moon and Jupiter appeared in the east. Listening to eulogies recited about Rama in Sanskrit, 16th-century poet Tulsidas rewrote the *Ramayana* in Avadhi. After all, Tulsidas was born in Gonda, near Lucknow. This way the majority of the population in the region that had not understood what was said in Sanskrit learnt to appreciate the marvelous times and life of Rama, and spread the word about the good man to an even wider world. There is a long period of which almost nothing is known after the story of Rama and Lakshman.

For several centuries Avadh was lost to wilderness, till tribals from the foothills of the mountains, like the Bhar by boat, and the Pasi by land, came to form kingdoms. To take the story forward, a visit to the remains of the Maharaja Bijli Pasi Qila in the Ashiana neighbourhood of Lucknow is a revelation. Bijli Pasi was a Dalit ruler in the 12th century. In the absence of written records, Bano Bua has to be believed when she says that Bijli Pasi built 12 forts, which speaks volumes of the power and wealth that the Pasi community must have wielded at that time. Bijli Pasi's kingdom was vast, and coveted for its fields overflowing with paddy, wheat, gram, peas, sorghum, and millet crops. Most jealous of Bijli Pasi's power and glory was Jaichand, ruler of Kannauj, who waged terrible wars against him. Today the Pasis are the second-largest caste among Dalits, after the Jatavs. They are spread across the central and northern parts of the province. The majority of Pasis do not have a formal education, and are left behind economically and socially by time. But they have remained fiercely independent. It is their defiant spirit that made the British fear them. In the late 19th century the colonialists officially dismissed the Pasis as a tribe of criminals, and only after the Criminal Tribes Act was repealed in 1952 were the Pasis declared a Scheduled Caste.

One piece of local lore says that Lucknow may have got its name from Lakhan Pasi, whose fort was once located on the same mound where the Machchi Bhawan came up later. Some Dalit records claim that parts of Avadh were ruled by Pasi kings between the 1st century and 11th century. The first Muslims must have come to Avadh with the army of Mahmud, who had many a Sheikh and Pathan in his employment.

Salar Ghazi, a nephew of Mahmud, was lured by the green fields of the plains of Avadh. His shrine in Bahraich is a pilgrimage place. His devotees believe that Salar Ghazi wanted to give up arms, but the local people begged him to first liberate them from the tyranny of a ruler called Suheldev. A battle was fought between Salar Ghazi and Suheldev in which both died. For local people Salar Ghazi is a martyr and his grave is a pilgrimage place for trying to fight on behalf of helpless people who were unhappy with their cruel king. But those who do not see Salar Ghazi as a friend hail Suheldev, a Dalit warrior king, as the hero who had tried to prevent Muslim armies from conquering Avadh. It may look like they are, but wars are not really over religion, but over land, property and wealth, between one group of warriors against another irrespective of religion.

KABIR DAS

I hope that Bano Bua will continue to be busy in some other part of the house. I must confess that her tinkling laughter fails to tickle me this twilight. I picture her looking for me everywhere. I just let her. Then a whiff of the perfume she uses, similar to the first drop of rain on parched earth, breezes in closer. Bano Bua's presence is a bouquet of fragrance from the last jasmine blossoms of the season, which she pokes into each earlobe every day. This sensory burden has barged upon my thoughts. She is now close to me, forcing me to smell her, be touched by her and hear her recite:

> The truant light again at play,
> Do I see it lurk behind dark tresses of the one I love,
> Or lost to sleep
> After a tiring day?

She places a glass of fresh lemonade beside me and, without waiting for me to respond to her overwhelming arrival, she walks with great confidence even in the dark towards the electric switch to click it down. The room is flooded with light from a 60-watt bulb.

I hear her wail. She has turned around to where I sit, and to look at what I have done.

"What have you done, Bibi? Why, Bibi, why...?"

She snatches from my hands the lily-white cloth, freshly woven by her, and one that she was still embroidering with more colours than in the rainbow. She holds it up wide open with both hands, wrings it out vigorously several times and then makes a curtain of it between herself and me. She is horrified to see how I have ruined the embroidery around a good corner of the three-metre long shawl.

"Bibi" is a word that both Hindus and Muslims use for "wife". But among Muslims "bibi" or "lady" is a diminutive word for "begum" or "female aristocrat", derived from the Turkic "*baig*" or "male official of great importance". "Bano" in Farsi also means "lady".

Bano Bua stamps closer, breathing fire. The touch of her bony finger on my lowered chin hurts. She jerks the same finger to raise my face, pressing me to look into her burning brown eyes. I do, through a well of tears dripping out of the eyes one drop at a time. I want to flood the floor with my tears and drench her rude shoving and pushing till she is reduced to a sinking sop.

She inhales and holds her breath. When she exhales the damaged white shawl drops from her hand and its multiple folds pile up in the middle of the room like a little mountain after a snowfall.

My tears have melted the hard expression on her face and her hands are now free to hold me.

"To hell with the shawl...I can weave another, another and another...Piece of my own heart, it is nothing. This shawl is zero. You, piece of my own life...forgive me. I am sorry," she coos.

"I am sorry...I did not mean to. I did not know what I was doing. It is not the shawl..." I sob.

"Never mind. Nothing matters except that you are happy. All that crying must make you bone-dry. It is enough for now. See, there is no liquid left in your body...you don't want to be reduced to a rattle, do you? Here, let me give you something to drink. Water is good for you," she says, stretching out to the glass of lemonade, putting it to my mouth. With one end of the shawl she wears she wipes my tears. But when she hears the knock on the door she is angry all over again. She sighs. She stamps a foot and tells me not to move till she returns. She marches to the door, I imagine in tune to the rhythm of the grinding of her own teeth.

"Then go on waiting. Have you forgotten how many times you made me wait for you while you took your time to oil your hair and to paint your eyes? No, I don't want to hear another word from you. Return to the rickshaw at once and wait there till we show up."

To hear Bano Bua speak in this tone is the best way to stop thinking of one's own hurt.

Poor Naresh, I think, and my tears dry up. Dabbing my face with my shawl, I run to the window to find Naresh walking back leisurely from the front door, through the garden path and towards the gate.

I lean as far as I can out of the window and shout, "Naresh, just a few minutes more. We are ready and will be with you soon."

I go into the bathroom but avoid looking into the mirror above the washbasin. I splash water on my face, run the comb through the top of my hair once, and I am ready to march out into the world with Bano Bua in search of Tulip Blossom.

Bano Bua goes to pieces when she sees me in pain. Now she pretends to be busy, walking nervously in and out of rooms, picking up this and putting down that, her shawl trailing behind her, her hair without a knot, the slippers on her feet mismatched. Of course Bano Bua was justified in losing her temper over the soiling of the shawl she was embroidering. Any activity associated with cloth making and embroidery means the world to her and to most people belonging to the traditional weaver families. Among weavers, an assault on any aspect of weft is like violence against life itself. Bano Bua taught me that and I regret having forgotten to respect the lesson. But to ruin any shawl was not the idea. It was just a mindless act.

Bano Bua traces Kabir, the weaver-poet from 15th-century Avadh, as her ancestor. Out of all the stories that Bano Bua tells me about Kabir, who in his own words was a child of both Allah and of Ram, I love this one the most. After he died, both Muslims and Hindus stood beside his body and fought over it. In the midst of the ugly argument, a stranger appeared before the crowd assembled to mourn the death of Kabir and asked the silly squabblers to lift the shroud and to look beneath it. When they did, they found a bed of flowers instead of a corpse. The devotees fell silent and quietly divided the flowers among themselves. The Muslims buried their share of the fragrance and Hindus carried theirs to Varanasi to cremate it.

Kabir is loved by millions of people to this day, as he was able to explain the invisible relationship between all creatures to each other and to the creator of the world. Kabir sang songs for humble human beings like craftsmen and peasants in their own language, using simple metaphors, including that of a loom. He took ideas that bewildered simple people and wove them into verses full of images and words familiar to those around him, even as he sat at a spinning wheel, trying to earn a living. He sang while he worked, wondering which thread he should match with what colour and which dye he should contrast with which tie. Kabir's weaving took inspiration from the creation of the master weaver or the super consciousness. He devoted his life to weaving cloth worthy of the human body, the most miraculous of all creation. A weaver marvels at the human body woven artfully around the spine. The backbone is a symbol of energy that connects Earth with the ethereal.

The opposing powers of the solar and lunar spheres electrify existence as it criss-crosses the spine in a figure-of-eight pattern. Inspired by creation and the beauty of nature and after much sweat and toil, when the cloth was finally finished, Kabir was careful not to soil it with sin or with soot.

Here is a translation by Rabindranath Tagore of one out of the thousands of love songs that Kabir had recited during a lifetime spent on the loom in Avadh in the 15th century:

> The woman who is parted from her lover spins at the wheel.
> The body of her shawl glows in beauty, designed with the palace of the mind here,
> And the chamber of heart there,
> What subtle threads the woman weaves,

Dyeing one with love and the other with reverence.
Says Kabir, I too weave a string of day and night, friends,
And when my lover comes I shall garland him with flowers soaked in tears.

MUNNA BHAI

Bano Bua says nothing during the rickshaw ride on the way to see Tamboli Begum. Once we reach the bottom of the bridge we are caught in a terrific traffic jam. There are the usual vehicles on the road, but the crowd of people is even larger than the ones that visit the weekly bazaars, held on different days in different neighbourhoods. Then vegetable, fruit and fake Rolex watch vendors spill their wares for sale beyond the pavement onto the main road.

"What is this? It is not even a Wednesday today. I don't know how we will ever make it through this crowd." Bano Bua looks around at the sea of people before us.

And as all of us crane our necks over the crowd, wondering how to wade through the human flood, we spy many black Mercedes cars in-between the usual Lucknow traffic of vehicles, animals and people. Bano Bua suggests that Naresh should park the rickshaw somewhere on the side of the road and find out the cause of the terrible traffic jam.

On the right-hand side of the bridge there is a dead end along the river. This road leads to Sahara City, a private little enclave built by Subrata Roy over 300 acres of prime land by the river. The palatial Sahara City has replaced some of the lost glory of the Kaiserbagh palace as the latest Disneyland in Lucknow. Sahara City is a second home for some film stars, politicians and business people. Subrata Roy, patriarch of the multibillion-dollar Sahara Group of businesses, had once owned a domestic airline and television network, and is also remembered for making rounds of the city on a bicycle. Just a few decades ago Subrata was ringing the bell before one door and then another, trying to sell tickets for a mutual fund. The entrepreneur's phenomenal rise to the statuses of a neo-nawab and Lucknow's most affluent man is the talk of town.

Naresh tries to take us on that road. But he notices that all traffic is blocked from turning right. A gigantic gate prevents Naresh from taking us to our favourite road along the cleanest part of the river.

This temporary gate reaches up to the heavens and is studded with neon lights that blink, that wink at us, but refuses to allow us to pass through. Only the black Mercedes cars zip in and out of the great gate.

Now, we are most unfamiliar with this kind of inhospitality. In the past we were aware that beauty queens and actors who made millions of hearts throb worldwide came to party on the premises of Sahara City. But the presence of glamorous guests inside Sahara City did not prevent the likes of Bano Bua and myself from enjoying a walk on the public road, even pausing to admire Sahara Palace from the outside and the way it glittered in shocking pink at twilight like a contemporary jewel in the city's rusting crown.

This evening is different. Perhaps it is not just another party. We want to know what it is. The excitement in the air is quite infectious.

"Naresh, go straight ahead to Munna Bhai. We can ask him to make us a cup of tea and tell us the meaning of this madness on the road today," suggests Bano Bua.

"I will park the rickshaw here, Bua. Let me walk you down to the tea stall instead," Naresh replies. We hop down from the rickshaw and walk behind Naresh, who resembles the biblical Moses in the way he keeps parting the sea of humanity to make way for us.

Munna Bhai stands outside his tea stall, smoking a cigarette. When he sees Bano Bua, he throws the stub behind his back and comes towards us, wearing a wide smile, to bend down and touch her feet. My presence inspires only a grin out of him.

"May God grant you a long life," Bano Bua blesses him.

Munna Bhai grins some more after Bano Bua tells him how we were held up by traffic and asks if he will offer us a cup of tea. Munna Bhai escorts us into the cubicle that serves as a place to eat and drink for people rich and poor. He wipes clean the bench and the wooden table below the only window within the enclosure with a wet sponge and switches on the table fan. The transistor radio is running but its music is overpowered by the deafening noise of the traffic outside. The place is modest but clean, and I cannot wait to sip tea.

Munna Bhai's daughter was recently engaged to a young man with a decent job in Dubai. Bano Bua had organised the marriage and ever since then she has been treated like a god in disguise by Munna Bhai. And Bano Bua is only too pleased to pretend that she is one.

About three decades ago Munna Bhai did not have such unattractive teeth. Then he had worn a crown of curly black hair and smart clothes. In fact, he was quite a lovely looking lad. Munna Bhai is a Lucknow University alumnus. He is from a family of scholars from Firangi Mahali that developed a curriculum in logic and philosophy in the 17th century as part of Islamic studies. He was also popular at the postgraduate department of the university for his fluency in both Urdu and English literature, at a time when it was feared that Urdu was a dying language.

All the romantics had found his princely presence on the Lucknow University campus transporting them to the early 19th century, when even ordinary citizens conversed in verse. In Badshah Bagh, where the university stands today, was a mango grove surrounded by trees and flower beds and used by the mysteriously reserved Bismillah as a nest, away from intrigues and the cunning of court. Bismillah was hired to the royal harem as maid to queen number two and in the presence of the king she was always veiled. Feeling playful one day, the then-ruler of Avadh threw a glass of water at her, soaking the veil into such transparency that he was thunderstruck at what was revealed to him.

The sight of her face made him faint with want and without her permission he buried his staggering self into Bismillah's bosom to announce her his eighth wife out of the nine women he ultimately married. In 1827 Fanny Parks wrote in *Wandering* that the king's wives were superbly dressed and looked like creatures of the *Arabian Nights*.

Bismillah's presence in his private chamber caused such envy that she was forced to disappear into the thicket of Badshah Bagh, a virtual paradise built by His Majesty at great cost. It was built in the heart of the city and was landscaped with fountains and tanks in marble. The tanks were filled with water, laced with the essence of pickled rose petals and curtained off with cypress trees. Here Bismillah was happy for a while, surrounded by an army of 500 female gardeners in uniforms that were embossed with a spade and axe emblem woven in gold thread over the right breast. But the dreamlike summerhouse of Badshah Bagh could not cool the fears of this commoner converted overnight to queen. One morning Bismillah committed suicide on the northern banks of the Gomti.

After having overpowered the armed rebellion against them in 1857, the British bombarded Badshah Bagh and reduced the latticed balconies and decorative pavilions to ruins, reinventing the pleasure garden into a rambling picnic spot for themselves. The colonialists destroyed not just Badshah Bagh but two thirds of everything in Lucknow that had made it one of the greatest cities of that time.

Emma Roberts, an English traveller, visited several parts of India including Lucknow in the 1830s and wrote:

> In no place can there be a more vivid realisation of the visions conjured up by a perusal of the splendid fictions of the *Arabian Nights*.

William Russell climbed on top of the Dilkusha Gardens when he came to the city two decades after Roberts as a war correspondent for *The London Times*. A glance to the west made him drool over the curves of the Gomti, the river responsible for making the flat lands so fertile. Before him he saw a lavish spread of groves and orchards of cypress, mango, orange, pomegranate, guava, custard apple, peach, nectarine, apricot and date palm, acre after acre of green foliage, reaching to the rim of the limpid sky. The sun found it impossible to keep its glittering eye away from the scattered domes, towers and parapets, fretted and curved, painted and gilded in-between the vegetation.

This was the Lucknow that Russell, perhaps the most well-known wanderer of his age, saw. He wrote:

> Not Rome, not Athens, not Constantinople, not any city I have ever seen appears to me so striking and so beautiful as this.

After Badshah Bagh was bulldozed, Canning College was built in its place in 1865. It was expanded in 1922 to include Lucknow University, the Arts College and the College of Music.

Lucknow was always an important centre of trade, but during the rule of Emperor Jahangir, its significance as a strategic place between Agra and Jaunpur, throne of the splendid Sharqi rulers, reached its peak. Lucknow was so protected by Delhi that a written permission to travel through the city was needed from none other than the Mughal emperor. When a French merchant arrived with a trade permit to live here for a year, he also built a home for himself and called it Frankish Palace. After the Frenchman left, his home became famous as Firangi Mahal and was used as a guest house by foreigners visiting Lucknow to trade in indigo, muslin and sugar.

Emperor Aurangzeb elevated Lucknow to a university town, and this grandson of Jahangir transformed Firangi Mahal into a seminary that in 1695 became famous as the Cambridge of Islamic Studies. Students came from China and Spain to sit at the feet of Firangi Mahal scholars to study Islam and lessons in reasoning and rationality. When citizens failed to get the British to retreat out of Lucknow in 1857, the Firangi Mahal scholars worried about the fate of Islam in a society influenced by so many new ideas from the West. From an open place of learning, Firangi Mahal became a home of insecure and conservative Muslim families. After 1947 most of the staff from Firangi Mahal migrated to Pakistan.

Although his ancestors did, Munna Bhai never lived in the conservative environment of Firangi Mahal, now fallen apart both in spirit and in cement. He grew up in Mahanagar, the cosmopolitan suburb of post-independent Lucknow, and was educated in the secular ambience of the La Martiniere Boys' College. On the university campus he was famous for his acting and singing abilities and for being able to quote Keats, Shelly and Wordsworth from memory, with as much ease as Majaz Lakhnawi's Urdu poetry, which I have translated from the original Urdu:

> The desire to loop the deadpan moon,
> Is to shatter it.
> As well as to smash the stars,
> To rip them from this end and to rip them from that end.
> Not to smash this one or just that,
> But to shatter them all,
> To rip them all.
> Now you tell me, my gloomy heart, what I should do instead,
> You tell me, heart of woe, what I should do instead?

And even before Munna Bhai touched the last lines of the poem by Majaz Lakhnawi called 'Vagabond', a few women in the audience would always faint out of concern of the socialist kind. Such was the poetic power of Munna Bhai.

In the mid-1970s Munna Bhai vanished. For a year no one knew what had become of him. While still a student, Munna Bhai had often loitered around the sleepy hamlet of Amausi, where the city airport is. To earn some pocket money, he waited for flights that sometimes brought tourists into Lucknow. He would offer his services to visitors as a city guide. Just before he was gone, he was seen chatting with a pair of foreigners.

A year later, when Munna Bhai reappeared in the city, people noticed that he had exchanged his Mona Lisa smile with a grin that was no enigma. He had forgotten all his poetry and somewhere on the way he had left behind the twinkle in his eye. There were rumours, but nobody got to know for sure what had happened. According to one version Munna Bhai was found buried neck down in snow in the mountains of Rishikesh when he was rescued. Another storyteller swears that Munna Bhai was found unconscious on a beach in Goa, covered in little else except gold sand, and lascivious waves had kissed him back to life.

One day Meera, an admirer of his from the university, walked up to propose marriage to Munna Bhai. When Munna Bhai asked her why, Meera replied it was because she was in love with him then, and in love with him now. Munna Bhai accepted the proposal and the two were soon married. Meera taught English Literature in a local school, and with part of the money that she had saved, she helped her husband open an eatery that was named the Munna Bhai Kebab Korner.

Meera also managed the kitchen. Munna Bhai's only responsibility was to take orders and the cash, and to deliver the kebabs over the counter. And if he forgot to perform all or any one of these three important tasks, someone always appeared from the kitchen to help him again. Some people did not mind sitting inside the crammed cubicle to eat, drink, talk and have a good laugh. Some others ordered food on the telephone and came a little later in a car to take away the most famous kebabs in town.

This is the life of Munna Bhai, a father of three now. A son studies computer science. The daughter will soon be married, and on her way to Dubai she will drop the younger brother in Mumbai, where he will star in his first Bollywood film. While giving us this information, Munna Bhai grins some more.

Bano Bua warns Munna Bhai that we did not like to eat except at home, and so when he parts the colourless curtain that hides all the kitchen's secrets from the guests, he returns with a tray with three cups of tea. The fumes that dance over the cups smell of cardamom seeds boiled together with a large spoonful of tea leaves, along with a good measure of milk and sugar.

MUHARRAM THEN AND NOW

I wait each year to witness the silent *matam* at the Grand Imambara, built by Asafudaulah on 300 square feet of land in the central well of the magnificent monument.

I remember the aunt who held me in her arms and periodically perched me as high as she could so I could watch human bodies clothed in black, tilted a little to the back and slapping the torso, first with the right hand and then with the left. The mourners did not need words to express their sorrow, letting the thudding rhythm resounding off thousands of breasts say it all.

"Why are these people hitting themselves? Why are these people hurting themselves?" I had wanted to know desperately from the aunt.

But she pushed me a little away from her to stare at me and say, "This is the moment of *matam*, Bibi. This is no time to be twittering. Now be quiet."

I looked away, throwing my own arms around her neck and shutting my eyes against her shoulder to sleep away my bewilderment.

Unlike all those who have tied themselves in tight knots to the world, it is much easier for a mystic to explain the overwhelming act of martyrdom in a matter-of-fact way. The Sufi sees self-flagellation as a desire to experience similar pain as endured by the beloved, and martyrdom as spiritual sacrifice, for a larger good.

"When a man's spirit is sacrificed, of what value are his wealth and his health and his frock and his food?" questions Ali ibn Uthman al-Hujwiri, an 11th-century Sufi author buried near Lahore.

I have also often heard Bano Bua sigh and wish that Shia Muslims would not observe the rituals at Muharram once a year but practice every day the courage and honesty Husain had shown in his life.

"So full of goodness was he. So perfect," says Bano Bua, her eyes almost always moist at the mention of Husain.

As long as my grandmother was alive, Muharram was the time of the year when members of the family, scattered in different parts of the country, returned home to the ancestral village. It was mostly the women who came regularly, accompanied by children who were happy to skip school for a few days, making the month a favourite time of the year for all.

The older children used the occasion to see how much better they were doing in life since the previous year, compared to cousins and neighbours. The women boasted to each other about their latest possessions, making others who had bought less during the year jealous. The competition among relatives made some sulk and stay away from the get-together, where all the poetry was recited in praise of Husain's goodness.

Overcome by emotions of their own, the jealous ones would busy themselves in showering verbal venom upon each other.

Watching our respective elders battle got us children excited, as each one of us cheered for one elder or the other from outside a window or from behind curtains. We hopped up and down in nervous excitement and in the hope that our favourite relative would emerge the winner of the day during the quarrels between families. The child whose elder was defeated was reduced to tears by the rest of us and made to feel like something that the cat had pawed. When I recall those games of victory and defeat, I experience the same pleasure as in childhood, but of late the feeling is accompanied by shame at the thought that I have enjoyed being so sadistic in the past.

Although everyone had collected to mourn the martyrdom of Husain, the occasion remained festive. The house often ran out of beds, but the kitchen never ran out of delicacies. Even on the 10th of Muharram, the saddest day of the month when Husain was killed and none were meant to think of drink or food, I could not help salivating at the thought of the next meal. I still love the *urad* lentil with the deep green skin cooked in the starchy, coarse and recently harvested rice on slow fire and served in clay plates no bigger than the palm of a hand. This simple but mouthwatering meal was served at sunset to mourners who had not eaten anything in 24 hours.

All the cots, woven in coir, were turned upside down for 10 days in the home as part of the annual mourning. To look at the cots lying upside down with their dark legs in the air was a surreal sight after sunset, even when the rooms were lit up with lanterns fed on kerosene oil.

On the eve of the first day of Muharram, the first month of the Islamic calendar, I would climb up the highest roof of the house, along with the women of the family, to watch them search the sky. As soon as the thin sliver of the new moon was spotted, the women uncovered themselves of all scarves and changed into black or green clothes in solidarity with the martyrdom of Husain. The women would also wail and let their hair tumble down the back in a deliberate attempt to look dishevelled. The body was stripped of all jewellery, from diamond nose rings to bracelets and anklets with a hundred bells. Glass bangles were dashed again and again against the edge of a low wall till they were strewn all over the floor like rainbows smashed to smithereens.

I don't think my grandmother's reputation as the grand dame of the city rested on her ability to sing or to recite. But that is not the point. Since she was the eldest, wherever we visited and in whatever we did as a group, she was expected to begin the *matam*, the act of lamentation when the breast is beaten with the palm of the right hand rhythmically. Then the *nauha*, the dirge, was recited (at the same time each year), in the same way and the same melody of the *Raga Jogiya*, composed by Wajid Ali Shah, the last ruler of Lucknow. After my grandmother had finished reciting the first line, the words were repeated by everyone, and together we chorused:

> There it is, the moon,
> That I spy.
> And hear the heavens cry,
> The first of Muharram
> Oh people!
> Is well nigh!

All of us beat our breast as we trooped down back through the dark well of the staircase, helped by lanterns struggling to flicker in adulterated kerosene oil. All the way to that corner of the house, converted into a temporary chapel for 10 days, on a dais that was draped in white cotton cloth and curtained in black, we continued to chant:

> Husain Imam, Husain Imam, Husaina,
> Masoom Imam, Masoom Imam, Masooma...

I would push my way to the front of the gang to admire all the memorabilia rolled out one by one from in-between the folds of perfumed muslin cloth and placed on a platform. I helped to decorate the sacred place created on the dais with the *panja,* a replica of the protective hand in beaten silver, with the names of Muhammad, Ali, Fatima, Hasan and Husain gilded on each fingertip. This hand guards against evil. There were several replicas of Zulfiqar, the sword of Ali, also in silver, placed beside banners or *alams,* arranged in a row atop tall poles symbolic of the flagstaff carried to battle by Husain and his army of civilians. Below this regalia were placed *tazia,* or replicas of tombs of all those martyred at Karbala, made of slim bamboo stick frames, over which tissue paper was stretched out by master craftsmen living in the old city of Lucknow, some of whom were Hindu. We were allowed to light as many candles as we liked before the grand pageantry. Unable to fully appreciate the content of the prose and poetry recited of events that led to the martyrdom of Husain in 7th-century Karbala in modern-day Iraq, and desperate to conform and join in the collective weeping around me, I would stare without blinking into the smoke from incense sticks and force tears to run down my face as well.

And any time that a wrong move was made at the chapel on the dais, hawk-eyed elders were quick to chide, "Oh, child of Yazid, that is not the way to do this."

Yazid ordered the massacre at Karbala from his throne in Damascus. After having killed the men, the forces of Yazid took the children and women of Husain's family and led them from Karbala to Kufa and finally to prisons in Damascus, the capital of Muslim power from where Islam spread east as far as South Asia and west to southern Spain.

Zainab, the sister of Husain, was beside herself with grief to see her brother's head laid out at the foot of Yazid's throne in Damascus. Her unkempt hair turned grey overnight and her back doubled up into a bow at the sight. In silence she had mourned in verse composed originally by a local poet, which I have translated here:

> My brother, how can I bring you back again?
> Whom do I tell about my pain?
> My world is changed beyond belief.
> It is impossible to breathe in this house of grief.

Zainab is remembered as a woman who was defeated but not destroyed. The poet imagines Zainab as someone who endured intense suffering but remained defiant as she held her head high and looked Yazid in the eye. The best storytellers in the family repeat the incident of Karbala in memory of Husain's martyrdom and quote Zainab:

> Is this justice? Oh son of freed slaves! You provide your women and slave-girls with cover but hold the daughters of Muhammad prisoner and insult them by mocking their modesty, by exposing their face to the enemy in one city then in another?

> Oh Yazid! Do you think that by taking us prisoner and parading us in public all over Arabia you can humiliate us in the sight of Allah, and earn respect for yourself?

The extravagant sparkle of Yazid's palace paled before the words of Zainab that day, and the tyrant stopped to tickle his pet monkey. A smirk, making its way to his face froze in flight, and quandary made Yazid stroke his beard, sprinkled with gold and silver confetti, and diamonds ground to dust. A hush dropped upon the wealthy merrymakers. The entire congregation of hundreds of courtiers looked to the floor and could eat and drink no more. Jesters were prompted to hold back their buffoonery and sycophants their breath, as they listened to the granddaughter of Muhammad speak.

> You are a ruler by force. You misuse your powers and oppress the people. You will have to kill me too if you touch my nephew.

Zainab said this, clutching to her breast 22-year-old Zainul Abidin, the ailing son of Husain, who had survived Karbala. Her own two sons, one 9 years old and the other 10 years old, had already been martyred along with Husain.

"And then what happened?" I would throw one question after another at my grandmother, refusing to sleep even when it was well past my bedtime.

"Whoever was still alive from the family of Muhammad was set free. Zainab led them to Medina, the city of the Prophet of Islam. Here people gathered around her in a majlis and she recounted for them the incident at Karbala as she had witnessed it and as she had experienced the tragedy," my grandmother repeated as many times as I was willing to listen.

And finally, when I did fall asleep on her fleshy arm, which I was allowed to use as a pillow, I would often dream of Zainab, seeing her wave aside the curtain of the tent at Karbala before it was set on fire by the enemy, her face unveiled, her chest heaving, her limbs trembling, her back bent, demanding justice for the family of the Prophet of Islam.

> Ah Karbala, is this the way of a host,
> My parched throat in pain?
> It will help most,
> If you get me to Husain.
> Under cover of desert sun,
> The daughter of Ali ran,
> To look for my father's son if I can.
> Dead to danger she drew near,
> To witness the brother's head dangled from spear.
> Could you bury me too beside my brother? she asked,
> Without tear.

Many believe that it is Zainab who saved Islam that day from the flames of Karbala. She had survived the tragedy and she made it a mission to let the world know exactly how the good grandson of Muhammad was denied water, deceived and killed in Karbala in an attempt to wipe out all direct descendants of the Prophet of Islam. In the same spirit, Shia households have been teaching their young ones for centuries never to deny water to anyone who is thirsty, especially a visitor.

Below the chapel at home, the rest of the floor was covered in a tapestry and in white sheets, with cushions strewn here and there. It was here that women from the family and from the neighbourhood collected every day to listen and to wail during the daily sermon at the majlis held by female champion narrators. Here, the events that led to the tragedy of Karbala beginning from the first day of Muharram were shared in verse and also in lyrical recitations. The women collected inside each other's homes every day till the martyrdom of Husain on the 10th day of Muharram to recite: "Every grain of sand groaned and tears of blood shed that turned the waters of the Euphrates red."

The men met for a similar majlis in the outer quarter of the house or at the mosque.

As for me, I spent most of the time at a majlis staring at Jamila Jan. I thought she was enchanting. I looked at her as she sat at the head of the congregation, her back to the chapel and her text resting on the floor on a low X-shaped stand carved out of wood. The audience looked at the chapel and at all the memento displayed there to help them imagine more vividly the tragedy in Karbala as Jamila Jan told them. But I had eyes only for Jamila Jan. In the shadow of lowered lights her face shone like the moon on the 14th day of the month. The lids took their time to curtain her almond-shaped eyes. Moments later when they were raised again I found her eyes filled with tears. After listening to her recite at majlis after majlis, day after day, I would go looking for the largest mirror in the house and stand before it to perfect my Jamila Jan look. Like Jamila Jan, I would try to coax the black shawl back to the head and down to the forehead, each time the truant chiffon slid down to cling to the nape of my neck. But the image was never right and with a sigh I would fling away my own shawl, concluding that there is no one who can ever be like Jamila Jan. Not even me.

Those moments were rare when I could look at Jamila Jan and also concentrate on what she said. I remember her explaining that it was on the second day of Muharram that thousands of soldiers had forced Husain to halt at Karbala and cut short his journey to Kufa. Husain was to pledge an oath of allegiance to Yazid, accepting the usurper as his leader. But how could the pious Husain agree to an alcoholic and debauch as a leader? Husain refused to do so. He wanted to proceed to Kufa, where the people waited for him to deliver them from Yazid, their oppressor. When confronted by the colossal army of the enemy, Husain had hesitated. Did he want to turn back from Karbala with his entourage of 72 members of his family and friends, and to leave the Muslim lands for good for some non-Muslim place, like India?

After posing this question, Jamila Jan denied that Husain may have thought this way. For an ordinary person could contemplate such an escape, but not Husain. He was no ordinary person. He was special. He was a visionary. He already had knowledge of his violent death. And he chose martyrdom. He chose martyrdom so that the tragedy would shake Muslims out of lethargy and wake them up to the moral threat faced by Islam.

Sentences like the last one were always drowned in a chorus of wails and beating of the breast by the congregation. After the sobbing of the faithful had subsided, Jamila Jan would continue.

The heavens watched Husain, the prince of Karbala, tiptoe out of the tent to eclipse the sun at twilight. He was careful not to wake up the children, who rested once the blistering heat of the day had passed. The fantasy of the poet took over as the audience was told how the night in the desert had welcomed Husain into its cool embrace. His presence had turned the wasteland into a wondrous land of twinkling dunes. If the poet is to be believed, invisible serenades wiped his sweat, and silken strokes cleared away creases of worry. Out of love for Husain, each star tried to shine brighter than the other to light up his path at the darkest moment of his life. The moon placed a kiss upon his brow.

Husain saw the Euphrates shimmer beyond; in-between him and the water stood the silhouette of thousands of soldiers. His throat was parched and he was thirsty but he was not there to plead for favours. He was in search of secrets that unravel silence. He concentrated on the voice within and was convinced that it was not possible to wipe out wickedness from the world merely by winning a war.

Then the heavens stood still. The first rays of the sun, along with the entire family of stars, the crescent of the moon, a little plumper this morning than the previous evening, witnessed Husain vow to face all the trials and tribulations before him in the spirit of Ali his father, and Muhammad his grandfather. Husain understood that the life given to him was not his own, that time keeps alive deeds and not just words in centuries to come.

He did not allow the deafening chants of "thirst, ah thirst" that escaped from the caravans sheltering thirsty women, children and elderly members of his family to weaken his will. Husain decided to sacrifice his life as a gift of hope to humanity. That hope is all that remains today. The hope that it is still possible to witness a world that is worthy of its creator.

Before the congregation could begin its painful roar again, Jamila Jan would raise the palm of her right hand, requesting a few more moments of patience and of silence from her audience.

By this time I was lost to reality. The surrounding and the sermon deceived me into mistaking the palm of Jamila Jan's hand for the silver *panja* from the chapel. I stared at it so hard that images of everything that I had just heard her say were projected upon it like a movie on a silver screen.

Sometimes I saw drops of blood trickle down the hand. There was Zuljuna, the horse of Husain, riddled with arrows, its mane soaked in blood, but it was still galloping, neighing. Zulfiqar was there, the sword of Ali and then of Husain that darted towards the enemy. I also sensed the presence of three women veiled in black. Maybe they were Fatima, the daughter of the Prophet and wife of Ali, with her daughter Zainab, and Sheharbano, the Persian wife of Husain and daughter of Khusrao Yazdigard III. The sombre sound of the kettledrum was seldom far and added drama to the rituals performed during Muharram.

Once the audience was quiet, Jamila Jan lowered her hand, but raised her voice to recite another verse that ended her sermon and also helped bridge the gap between the relevance of incidents that took place long ago in the past and life today.

> Every place is Karbala and every day is Ashura.
> Call the prince of Karbala,
> To look upon our century,
> At the tumult,
> Turmoil and tension.
> Today the number of Yazids is multiplied,
> Yesterday there was but one.
> In land after land truth is done,
> And human feet are in chain,
> Again.

Qamar Uncle was only one moth out of a hoard to gravitate to the flame of Jamila Jan's warm beauty. On his annual visits home from abroad he spent much of his time, like many others, hovering around Jamila Jan, knowing that the fire of desire could roast him at the snap of a finger.

One day I played hop, skip and jump in the courtyard while Jamila Jan sat on a cot woven in coiled jute in the verandah. She was surrounded by little baskets of various vegetables that she picked, cleaned and chopped with a knife.

"Let me take you with me, Jamila," I heard, and could not jump after the skip. Frozen still on one leg, I listened to Qamar Uncle, who lived in London but still talked like one from Lucknow, continue.

"If you refuse to marry me, Jamila, life is not worth living. I will kill myself here and now...with this." And he tried to snatch the kitchen knife from Jamila Jan's hand.

I tiptoed behind one of the many pillars that held the verandah high, similar to many more that ran around all the four sides of the square courtyard. My heart throbbing in great excitement, I listened without guilt.

"What are you doing? What if someone sees us? No! Give it back to me," I heard Jamila Jan's tearful pleas drown in the jingle jangle of dozens of glass bangles around her dainty wrists.

Then, swallowing a scream, with eyes wide open, I also saw Qamar Uncle hold the two ends of the collar of his embroidered shirt of white muslin cloth with each fist and tear it down to the bottom. Then he tore again to detach a smaller piece of cloth from the shirt and lowered his torso closer to the cot, his hairy chest bare and rubbing against the bowed head of Jamila Jan, whose shoulders shook as she sobbed soundlessly. When my own gaze lowered, I found blood escaping to the floor from in-between the zigzag patterns holding the coir cot together, drop by drop. I went down on my haunches to watch the dribble become a large circle, much larger than the *sheermaal,* a popular bread dipped in saffron. When I could watch no longer, I let out a shrill cry of such horror that a flood of people from different directions poured down the stairs, trickled in from the outside and streamed in from the neighbourhood in curiosity and concern.

Jamila Jan did marry Qamar Uncle, and travelled with him to London. Later they moved to Chicago, where Qamar Uncle got involved with another woman, then another, and then another. But the community of Shia Indian Muslims in Chicago refused to let Jamila Jan return to Lucknow to her widowed mother and younger siblings. She was wanted by the Shia living in the USA to recite the majlis for them, at first only in Chicago, then all over the country. Her mother now lives with her. I watched a video of Jamila Jan's sermons and recitations recently taped by someone we know who lives in Australia.

MUHARRAM AND A MARRIAGE

I wait to step out of Munna Bhai's Kebab Korner and find myself straying into a crowd. I pull back, and from a position frozen by the wooden frame of the door I look for Bano Bua. But the glow from the three-day-old moon is too dim to help me figure out who is who in the multitude. I peer into my wristwatch. In the semi-darkness I barely recognise that it is already the beginning of another day and that we are stranded in a blackout.

I can hardly see, but feel that everyone is waiting for something to happen. I imagine people standing on one leg and then on the other, trying to yawn and to speak at the same time. Some stretch out their limbs and air the armpits while others furiously scratch a crotch itching in sweat. Together they slap bugs that try to feed on the exposed parts of their respective bodies. Collectively drenched in copious quantities of perspiration, the crowd wipes itself continuously with their shirts. I am so sure that those out there on the street are mostly men.

Considering that such a large number of people stand before me, the atmosphere is unusually controlled, especially in the absence of fumes and noise made during the day by automobiles and the hurry and scurry of human beings on the go. In the hush of the night the exchange between people is reduced to a more monotonous, low hum, except for the clear lament of the travelling voice that gets closer.

I listen to a single beat mark time upon a kettledrum that is chained around the abdomen of probably the most muscular Shia Muslim around. Accompanying the drum is a chorus of voices of people surely dressed either in black kurtas or similar knee-length tunics in green. Everyone in the group probably uses the body as well as the metronome, hitting the chest with the right hand in rhythm to the melody. Some might use both hands one at a time to beat their breast in tune to what they repeat after the lead singer. I cannot see the people, but as I concentrate some more I recognise the music they make. Then the lyrics bubble out of memory to trickle down my voice and I find myself repeating in silence:

> The waters are stormy,
> The shore is not near.
> Evil will have us forget,
> And to dry our tears.
> But we mourn Husain,
> Our leader so dear.
> We remember the heat,
> And the dust of Karbala,
> Where he battled without retreat,
> No water,
> And not a drop of fear.

It occurs to me at that moment that it must be Muharram. It has been ages since I last looked at the lunar calendar to check dates for performing Islamic rites and rituals, taught to me by my grandmother. Although Bano Bua remains a spiritual person, I feel she prefers now to converse with her creator in the privacy of her bedroom. When she gets restless I have noticed that she seeks solace at the cave of the Baba of the Bottles, but seldom at a mosque. But during conversations about religion, she still insists that we Shia are a special community of people who continue to pine for the true spirit of Islam that has never been practiced except by Muhammad.

"To this day, the only quality that the Shia look for in a leader is virtue," Bano Bua tells me. Followers of Ali like her believe that only the virtuous can lead others, and if the leader goes astray, obedience should be withdrawn from him. True believers are even encouraged to revolt against the non-virtuous and to never give up trying to create a just society.

"And therefore the Shia are a minority, like all good things on this earth," Bano Bua is quick to point out with a playful curl of the mouth, but accompanied with a shadow of sorrow in the eyes.

It is true that the Shia are only about 15 per cent of the world's one billion Muslims. They usher in the Islamic New Year with a peculiar kind of joy. During Muharram, the Shia celebrate the victory of virtue over death with tears and with self-flagellation in public. They create a little Karbala, a holy place symbolic of pain or *karb* on trial, or *bala,* wherever they might be scattered in the world. They spend the entire month and 10 more days remembering Husain, martyred in 680 in the desert of southern Iraq on the orders of a cruel ruler.

"To further torture him, the waters of the Euphrates were cut off exactly at the spot where Husain had pitched his tent in Karbala," Bano Bua told me once as we searched for something to drink one scorching summer evening, even as the waters of the Gomti glistened behind us. We had been sitting on marble steps that lead up from the river bank to the tall tower of the martyr's memorial, built for all the unknown soldiers who died on the battlefield.

"But instead of compromising, Husain chose to defy the devil and refused to retreat. He was killed before the people could be liberated from tyranny," Bano Bua had continued, offering me a cone made from an old newspaper, filled with chickpeas that were soaked, flattened, drenched in spices and deep-fried. This is a favourite snack precisely because it is able to tease the palate and bring tears to the eyes.

Before his journey to confront the tyrant, Husain had exempted all his followers from the obligation of travelling with him. But the women and children of his household came with him to Karbala, perhaps to shock Muslims at the humiliation and captivity of innocent members of the Prophet's family by the wicked. Husain wanted Muslims to return to the Sunna, to the pious way of Muhammad. Husain wanted to inspire Muslims to stand up to injustice without wanting anything in return. By sacrificing his life and endangering the safety of the women of his family, Husain hoped to increase humanity's aversion to all kinds of tyranny.

The first Muslims had marched out of their dusty homes in the desert in the 7th century to conquer the more fertile lands of modern-day Syria, Iraq, Iran and Afghanistan. Muslims had thundered on their Arab steeds down the Himalayas into India as well. A group of Muslims broke away from mainstream Muslim monarchs. The rebels called themselves the Shia, the friends of Ali. The Shia keep alive the memory of Ali as Imam, the first leader of the community after Muhammad, and to this day revere the direct descendants of the Prophet's family as *ahlul bayt* or divine beings. They continue to mourn the fact that Islam is not practiced the way it should be. Over the years, they have perfected a culture of grief around the incident of Karbala as protest against the depraved ways of most Muslim leaders responsible for destroying democratic institutions introduced so religiously into tribal Arab society by Muhammad. When the Arabs conquered their lands in the 7th century, the Persians mourned. This grief mingled with the tragedy of Karbala and Muharram seemed like an apt occasion to manifest all that made the Persians so sad.

The path of the Shia turned towards Lucknow when many soldiers of Persian origin were assigned subordinate jobs to the city by the Mughal rulers of Delhi. Over time the Persians surfaced as Lucknow's most dazzling elite. In the 18th century, Lucknow won autonomy from Delhi, providing the city's Shia aristocracy complete independence. Now it could make a grand public display of the mourning period during Muharram. Processions were encouraged to parade down the streets of the city with the blessings of Shia religious scholars trained in law schools in Persia.

When Asafudaulah moved his capital from Faizabad to Lucknow, he first built not a pleasure palace for himself, but an extraordinary *imambara* for the Shia to congregate in, especially during Muharram.

The Asafi Imambara is an awesome structure with a gigantic inner chamber, crowned with a vault that stands without the conventional support of pillars or beams, its weight balanced by a series of arcs. Above the hall are seven entrances with decorative terraces and arches capped with small domes, creating the effect of fine filigree when viewed from a distance. The labyrinth with 489 identical doorways and a pathway designed like the inside of a honeycomb is a place where people from different walks of life amuse themselves by getting lost there on a leisurely Sunday afternoon. The *imambara* shares its premises with a triple-onion-domed mosque flanked by tall minarets, also built by Asafudaulah. Within a decade of his arrival he made Lucknow one of the most important cities of the Shia way of life.

In Islam the idea of God is an abstract one. God is remembered by attributes like benevolence and mercy. Any earthly manifestation of God is strictly forbidden. However, when the Persians came to Lucknow, they were curious about local customs, rites and rituals. They observed the way people worshipped, and discovered that the relationship between the deity and devotee is darshanic. Homage is paid not just to the abstract idea of the creator of the world but to a figurine of the one adored. And the devotee does not shy away from looking at the object of adoration in the eye. It did not take long for the city's rulers of Persian origin to indulge in similar worship of numerous replicas of their own, inviting Hindus to join them in observing Muharram in Lucknow.

I know Aunty Nigam from next door liked to come to every majlis at home, although she is not Shia. She is not even Muslim. She did not beat her breast or copiously cry on cue during the sermon, but she did remember to wear clothes that were dyed in subdued colours, and listened to the narration of the incidents at Karbala in silence. She was unlike some other women from the family who were routinely interrupted and told not to gossip in the back rows of the congregation.

As I got older and realised that Aunty Nigam is Hindu, I was tempted one day to ask her why she chose to mourn with us during Muharram.

"Because of friendship," she replied promptly.

"I have known your grandmother since we were 15 years old. We may be born from the womb of two women but I love her like I do my sister," she said, wiping her tears with the pallu of her sari.

Before she moved on to talking about other things she added with a wink, "It is not for God that I visit your house at Muharram, but for the love of your grandmother."

It is pleasant to engage in this kind of conversation, especially in Lucknow, where it is considered rude to talk frankly about matters that matter most. The thought of Aunty Nigam takes me to memories of my grandmother, who is one person I hold responsible for tutoring me to keep certain thoughts to myself.

"Always think before you say anything," she was to repeat so often that it made me tongue-tied for life. By the time I finish thinking, I notice that it is too late to say what I want to. The formula obviously does not work the same way with me as it did with my grandmother, who had followed up her thinking with speech that was considered most appropriate. Or was it?

Here is an example from a long time ago, when she could have said more but chose not to. My grandmother's English tutor had taught her never to forget her wedding anniversary. One morning I heard her ask my grandfather to promise that he would be home for dinner that evening. I did not hear him ask her why, and she did not tell him the importance of the date.

Then he left as usual for the Roshanudaulah Mansion, home of the city's lower court of justice. Once, the mansion was the residence of Roshanudaulah, the wily minister of Nasiruddin Haidar Shah, the ruler of Lucknow till 1837. Here dozens of people waited each day, expecting to receive justice from officials like my grandfather. My grandmother had spent that entire morning in the kitchen. She hummed to herself and let me help her grate the almonds and tuck them into the hollow stomach of a spring chicken. She got the cook to assist her to roast and paste the sesame seeds, deep-fry and grind the onions, crush the garlic and ginger, squeeze out juice from the lemons, and stir in a pinch of turmeric and salt whipped together. This was an exotic mix meant to replace the organs of the lynched bird. But she insisted on laying out the chicken on its back in a yoghurt sauce herself and kept a loving eye on the oven till mere bird metamorphosed into a splendid dish of *murg musallam* and it became impossible to tell bone from flesh.

But morn turned to noon and slid into twilight. There was no sign of my grandfather till perhaps the wee hours of the next morning. He came home only after my grandmother had donned her cotton night clothes. The finery in chiffon worn by her earlier in the evening, after a leisurely massage in precious olive oil brought to her from Istanbul, was folded back into the cupboard. Even at that hour she was still wide awake, while I only pretended to be asleep.

"Where were you for so long?" she asked in a not-too-unfriendly way.

"There," he replied as he sat down to take off his shoes and then his clothes.

"You promised to have dinner at home."

"Yes."

"Have you eaten?"

"Yes."

"With whom?"

"With them."

"Don't you remember at all?"

"What?"

"Have you never remembered in all these 50 years?"

"What?"

Then in a gesture that broke my heart my grandfather's figure disappeared into the bathroom, as if he had lived through just another day. I reached out to my grandmother to beg softly into her ear, "Why don't you tell him? Please remind him..."

"This is something that we should both remember on our own. Only then does it have the meaning it is meant to have. It is not enough for just one person to consider something important that requires two people to do so," she said, looking at my face so full of concern with a big smile. I found not a hint of self-pity or annoyance in her voice.

Looking into her eyes at that hour I was overcome with a surge of great strength. The most precious legacy that a child can inherit from an elder then is the assurance that you can take care of yourself under all kinds of circumstances, irrespective of however heartbreaking they may be. After having told me what she did, she stretched out a hand to switch off the light on her side of the bed. I snuggled closer to her with the thought that her relationship with her husband was so unfair. In my mind's verdict, my grandfather's priorities were pathetic. I was so proud of my grandmother's attitude of the moment. Yes, the relationship between a wife and husband involves much more than being married, like also being considerate towards each other. Since my grandfather showed little consideration towards his wife, my grandmother taught herself that whatever her husband did or did not do for her was not the end of the world. This way she was able to enjoy other bounties life offered her, as much as she could.

Life in Lucknow is special perhaps because many citizens like my grandmother have lived by example. Although taken to an extreme, the practice of such carefulness also discourages people from openly talking about things that matter most to them. For the same reason I never found out why I loved going into Aunty Nigam's prayer room. I did that not only during a Hindu festival but whenever I felt like sitting with legs crossed to stare in silence at the figure of Krishna—draped in tassels of gold and silver—so inseparable from the flute forever playing between his lips. I have sung many songs describing the ecstasy experienced in adoring the child-god as mischievous as mortals and more mysterious than Morpheus.

THE WHO'S WHO OF AVADH

Many a Buddhist from China had passed through Avadh even before the Europeans came. They were ecstatic at the thought of walking in the footsteps of the Buddha, who spent many years wandering in Avadh. Afghan fighters had constantly camped in Lucknow ever since the sultans of the Slave dynasty began their rule in 1206 in Delhi. Before the Afghans and the Turks came the Greek traders and warriors. Every conqueror has come to Avadh in the hope of confiscating the granaries overflowing with a rich variety of cereals. Nasiruddin Mahmud, sultan of Delhi and governor of Avadh, came in the 13th century, following Iltutmish, his father, who had built grand baths at Hauz Khas in Delhi. The pastoral beauty of the plains had so overwhelmed poet Amir Khusro in the same century that he composed many verses there. Khusro was at his best when he sang in praise of the endless spread of mustard fields carpeted at the feet of fruit-laden green trees that contrasted deliciously with the red flower known as the flame of the forest. Part of the psychedelic panorama were numerous belles dressed in colours as if out of a prism, their jewellery nudging and winking wickedly under the naked gaze of the sun, who went about their daily chores on Earth without care for the poet's stare.

Born in the western part of Avadh to a Turkic father and Indian mother, Khusro is one of the greatest poets of all time. He wrote endlessly about the beauty of the countryside that he was in. In his poems he marvels at the shameless splash of colours in nature and at the constant coo of the cuckoo.

Muhammad bin Tughlaq marched through Lucknow in the 14th century in the company of Ibn Battuta, the Moroccan adventurer who was fascinated with the betel leaves offered to him there. Ibn Battuta notes in his book of travels that *gilauris*, or carefully folded betel leaves, prepared for chewing, is an ancient Indian custom. When favours and rewards were given, betel leaves were also served at court. When a ruler wanted to give an important task to an official, he would offer a *gilauri* wrapped in silver paper and laid out on a tray in gold and ask, "Who will accept this?"

Whoever stepped forward to own the *gilauri* became responsible for the official task at hand.

Zahiruddin Babur, the Farsi-speaking Mongol who founded the Mughal dynasty, heard of the riverine riches around Lucknow soon after he conquered South Asia in 1526. Babur then battled in 1528 with Bayazid Farmuli, an Afghan chief, near Lucknow. After Babur's sudden death in 1530, Sher Shah Suri, another Afghan general, defeated Humayun, Babur's son and successor, in 1540, in one more battle nearby. Humayun found immediate refuge in the city. After some rest, and many melt-in-the-mouth meals, he left Lucknow for Persia with generous donations from people there, who also gifted him cattle for his survival. Humayun lived in exile in Persia for the next 15 years of his life, till it was safe for him to return to Delhi as the second Mughal emperor.

Humayun's son Akbar consolidated the sprawling lands, divided into warring fiefdoms, into Avadh. This is a Persianised variation of Ayodhya, a word that the British could pronounce only as Oudh. Babur had jealously guarded Lucknow in the late 1520s, after he heard that mercenary German soldiers had set Rome ablaze and were willing to perform the same job in any part of the planet for a price. Michelangelo Buonarroti gave up drawing to fortify the hill of San Miniatto and to defend Florence, his beloved city. He moved to Rome to sing sonnets to Lady Vittoria Colonna when Humayun took refuge in Lucknow in 1539 from his enemies.

Akbar the Great was delighted to watch the revenue from the fertile fields around Lucknow fill his treasury. He ordered that the royal mint for moulding copper and silver coins be built here. The emperor made friends with Hindu priests and made generous donations to the community of Brahmins in Lucknow, who promised to perform sacred ceremonies to assure that the fertile lands of the region would remain his. Akbar's visit to Lucknow is immortalised by a gate built on the southern side of Chowk, the old city that was the centre of all activity at that time. In the vicinity of Akbar Gate, with arches sweeping generously over raised verandahs, lies the tomb of Mir Babar Ali Anis, a 19th-century Urdu poet who broke away from images of wine and women, so popular with poets of his time, to explore ideas of life and death in his own inimitable way, translated here from the original Urdu.

> The mouth-watering taste of silence here,
> The eyes shut but vision clear.
> No quarrel with friend, no fight with foe,
> What a strange place is the tomb to go.

When local leaders refused to pay revenue to Delhi, it made the Mughal rulers want Lucknow even more. Shah Jahan, the Mughal ruler who built the Taj Mahal close to Lucknow, imagined the eastern lands of his empire to be closest to Shiraz, that Persian city of roses and poets, and the birthplace of Hafiz, the 14th-century bard who wrote:

> For many years my heart wanted
> Something for me,
> Not knowing that it was itself,
> What it wanted.

In 1707, on the death of the Mughal emperor Bahadur Shah Zafar I, the third son of Aurangzeb became king. He followed the Shia path of Islam. When Muhammad Nasir, a Shia aristocrat of Nishapur, got news of this in faraway Persia, he promptly packed his bags and came to Delhi. This Persian belonged to a family of well-known merchants whose ancestors had worked in the court of Emperor Shah Jahan.

Nasir's son, Muhammad Amin, was appointed governor of Avadh and called Saadat Khan. He left Ayodhya and founded a twin city Bangla, later called Faizabad. He brought to book rebellious feudal lords and founded the Shia dynasty of Lucknow, which reigned supreme till 1856, after which the tide of the oceanic generosity of the rulers itself turned against them. Once he had consolidated his power in Avadh, Saadat Khan adopted two fishes as his royal emblem. The experience of having lorded over vast stretches of land and people from Greece to Siberia added mystique to the Persian's personality. When the Persian came to Avadh he brought many a mystery with him from his land of origin, including Shia practices of *Islam-i-Ajam* that took root here and flowered in Avadh's lush landscape and the largess of its population. The Persian is remembered also for his polite diplomacy and love of poetry. It is a matter of much thrill to hear master *dastango* Bano Bua sing praises of him compared to my own poker-faced narration about our shared past. To be audience to Bano Bua when she is partial to everything Persian is to see her eyes travel far away, to watch her hands speak and to experience her entire body open up quietly to an enchanting, inner excitement. The fertile fields of the plains had made the Persians fight with each other over Avadh. Once the lush land was conquered by Persians they thought of unusual ways to consolidate their power. At the peak of his glory the Persians questioned their own need to make a home in Lucknow. The Persians looked for support from the majority of people, who looked up to them as their leader.

The Persian taught himself to respect the wishes of other people. He observed the ways of the population. He wondered how he could provide for those who had nothing without humiliating them to beg him for what was their birthright. He tried to anticipate the needs of others. He was aware that power was with a small community of people belonging to Islam while the majority of people were not Muslim. He recalled how humiliating it was to be defeated by the 7th-century Arab armies, who destroyed everything that Zarathustra had taught Persia in Avadh. The Persian looked around at all the land he had conquered and felt responsible for all the people who lived on this territory. He saw the river but resolved to continue his search for the ocean, for water that would quench the fire of anger, greed and jealousy, for glass that would crack stone, for prayer that would change the world, for a companion who would help him preserve faith in himself.

He began by attracting the attention of the people. He dismounted from his high horse. He touched the fingers of his right hand lightly to the left side of his chest as if to tap his heart to open up a little more and swept into a low bow in an expression of humility. The salutation was in celebration of the presence of others and the sublimation of the self in the other person in the same spirit as "namaste", that local greeting of bringing the palms of the hands together and bowing down. The same hand now moved to his forehead to greet one and all with *adaab*, from *adab* or "culture" or "respect for the other".

This act of disarming those who threaten, or feel threatened, later became the backbone of the way of life here. In fact, what else can the sensitive one do but muster up all the wit and poetry at his command, especially in moments of deep despair, or absolute victory?

Like Omar Khayam, the son of a tent-maker also from Nishapur, Persia turned to poetry for solace after it was unable to protect itself in the 7th century from Arab armies that introduced Islam to the Persians. The Persians resisted but failed to prevent Islam from vanquishing them. The toughest battle was to conquer their own emotions of sorrow and revenge after their defeat and to concentrate on ideas of love, life and poetry. The vanquished were forced to accept the new faith, which they decided to practice in a unique Persian way. By the early 12th century the Persians had reconciled to their fate and poet Omar Khayyam was inspired to pen an entire rubai in praise of Muhammad, introduced to him by his Arab conquerors.

> The mighty Muhammad, the victorious Lord,
> That all the misbelieving and black horde
> Of fears and sorrows that inflict the soul
> Scatters and slays with his enchanted sword.

After accepting and praising Muhammad, the Persians reinterpreted Islam to accommodate their own yearnings. Ali, the cousin, closest companion, son-in-law of Muhammad and the most rebellious of all Arabs, became the Shia or friend of the Persian. When Islam came to Avadh it was *Islam-i-Ajam* that became most influential here.

For every argument of *Islam-i-Arab,* the *Islam-i-Ajam* imagined his own view of the world. Muhammad is indeed the messenger of God and the last Prophet, but the memory of Ali is elevated to first Imam by the Persian. The mosque is a place of worship but the *imambara* too is a place of sacred congregations. After having lost their faith to conquerors, the Persians fought tooth and nail to keep their culture and language alive. Firdausi, the Persian poet, died in 1020 after spending 35 years of his life collecting tales of heroic characters from pre-Islamic times. He went from village to village to listen to elders and master storytellers talk about life along the twin rivers Tigris and Euphrates before Arab soldiers founded Baghdad.

When Firdausi felt he had all the information he needed to write about the way the Persians were before they were conquered by the Arabs, he wrote *The Shahnama* so that pre-Islamic Persia would never be forgotten. Firdausi wrote a 60,000-line poem in Farsi in 1010 in praise of Zoroastrian heroes like Rustom and Sohrab. The stories are popular even beyond the borders of modern-day Iran. Bollywood made a film in 1963 called *Rustom aur Sohrab,* starring legendary actors Prithviraj Kapoor and Suraiya.

Medieval Muslim rulers encouraged religious texts in Arabic to be translated into Farsi. The Persians enriched their language by including Arabic vocabulary. Day-to-day affairs of public interest were recorded in Farsi, now written in the Arabic script. Arabic remained the language of scholars and of theology, but Farsi was spoken by the people, and poets continue to connect the heart of one human being with another in this sweet language.

With a remarkable history like this, it was not possible for Saadat Khan to just barge into Avadh as if he was a barbarian conqueror. Look at the way he faced opposition in Lucknow. When the influential Sheikhs in the city refused to invite him into the Machchi Bhawan, he camped in one corner of the crowded marketplace near Chowk. He spent his time making friends with the people on the street and won over the tinker, tailor, and soldier in the Urdu language. After he had made himself sufficiently understood, he organised an impressive feast. The Sheikhs were invited by Saadat Khan to be guests in their own city, but in his camp. He employed the best cooks, and chose the most coveted women in Chowk for company. Once he had his guests engaged in merrymaking, Saadat Khan slid away to cross the river in a boat that waited at the Gaughat quay. He met the contingent of military men sent by Delhi and led them into the fortified citadel of the Sheikhs in the silence of a night without a moon. As he had rowed nearer to the Machchi Bhawan, two fish danced out of the water and fell into his lap. The boatman told him that this was a good omen. That this was the only way a fish knew to welcome him in Lucknow.

The fish in his lap reminded Saadat Khan of the *Mahi Maratib,* the Order of the Big Fish so dear to the heart of ancient Persian rulers. Fishes are an auspicious symbol in Persian mythology as the first sign of life. Among Mesopotamians the belief was that early civilisation was founded by human beings who had emerged out of the sea in the form of fish.

Saadat Khan caressed the fish fondly and slipped it back into the river before stepping out of the boat. He docked below the Lakshman Tila and galloped into the Machchi Bhawan on a horse already harnessed for him by a pair of anonymous hands that obviously wished him well. Without fight he walked through the main portal and by the time the Sheikhs caught up with him, he was ready to receive the opposition on its own turf with an *adaab.* He returned to the Sheikhs the dreaded sword that had hung above the main entrance of the fort in its sheath. Saadat Khan captured the courtyards and the inner chambers of the fort as well, but at the end of the military operation he returned to rest at the *ordu,* his own encampment in Chowk, enriching his vocabulary with new words for a few more days from the sounds that he heard around him. During the reign of Saadat Khan and his descendants in Avadh, it did not take long for Urdu to perfect itself as one of the most attractive languages this side of the world.

Nearly 300 years after the arrival of Saadat Khan in Avadh, Urdu blossomed into a lush language best reflected in the work of Faiz Ahmad Faiz, perhaps one of the most lovable poets of the 20th century.

Here is a translation by me of a poem by Faiz from the original Urdu:

> You stay with me,
> My sweet ruin, my life,
> Stay with me
> When night visits,
> High on sky's blood,
> With balm of musk, in dazzling, double-edged dress.
> When night approaches reciting, giggling, humming,
> Jingling anklets blue with pain,
> When hearts drowning in breasts,
> Look for hands folded in sleeve
> Full of hope.
> Wine froths in bottle like a child's breathless cry unconsoled,
> For solace,
> And finds none.
> When nothing resolves,
> When nothing works,
> When night works,
> When lamenting, silent, dark night visits alone
> Stay with me,
> My sweet ruin, my life
> You stay with me.

The sun eventually set over the empire of *Islam-i-Ajam* to reverse the wheel of fortune for Muslims around the world. *Islam-i-Arab* enjoys better economic clout today due to massive reserves of crude oil discovered in their land in recent times. There are many more job opportunities to be found in the Arab world than in the world of the Ajam. The influence of *Islam-i-Ajam* is no longer strong in Avadh, and the Arabic *allah hafiz* is heard much more than the Farsi *khuda hafiz*, and *salam alaikum* more than *adaab*. People from Lucknow travel to Arab lands to earn a living. They leave the city with a *khuda hafiz* but return saying *allah hafiz*. *Khuda* is the Farsi word for God and *allah* is the Arabic word for God. While *salam alaikum* is a greeting in Arabic, *adaab* is one in Urdu, a language patronised by Persian rulers and born among soldiers from different parts of the world who had camped in the *ordu*, or cantonments, in North India nearly a thousand years ago.

Muhammad, who spent his life trying to unite and bring peace among warring tribes of the Arabian Peninsula in the 6th century, was a Hashim, part of an Arab tribe from the Hijaz, that great wall between the Arabian Peninsula and the Red Sea. The present-day ruling family of Saudi Arabia is from Najd, from the plateau to the north of the Hijaz.

The families of the Hijaz and Najd have a long history of rivalry. The house of Saud follows the Wahhabi school of Islam. That is alright. What is unfair is the imposition upon Muslims everywhere of that single interpretation of Islam according to Abdul Wahab, an 18th-century Islamic scholar and spiritual soulmate of the patriarch of the Saudi family.

The rule of the Shia in Lucknow was indeed magnificent, not only for the initial magic of its military or for the panache of its politics, but also as a great experience in spirituality and creativity. During this time the opulence of the court had flooded the streets and the commoner had spouted poetry often superior to the king's, to the utter delight of His Majesty, of course. The Shia rulers of Lucknow were indeed unique, but they could not hold on to their way of life forever. The extravaganza built up so breathlessly by the rulers of Avadh collapsed when grotesqueness got garbed as goodness and springtime soirees were dragged into winter without care for the desire of autumn. A time so bizarre came to pass in town when more fins, one more fancy than the other, than actual fish in the Gomti were found plastered on walls in Lucknow.

Whatever Bano Bua may say about the sophistication of Asafudaulah, he is also remembered by his contemporaries as somewhat uncouth of appearance. His love for pleasure was obvious. He was a bundle of generosity, shrewdness, vanity and inertia. Faiz Bakhsh, a contemporary chronicler, observes in *Tarikh-i-Farahbaksh*:

> His features bore a general resemblance to his father's. The upper part of his body was rather long, but the lower part from waist downwards was very short. From childhood he was obese; his fat ears, neck and double chin were one fleshy mass. His fingers and palm were short and plump. From his boyhood he was addicted to frivolities and his natural inclinations and attachments were for low, ill born and base-minded associates. He used to laugh unseasonably, fling derisive abuse at others and desire derisive abuse in return. He delighted in meaningless amusements and was immensely pleased with anyone who indulged in filthy language, and the more obscene the conversation was in any company the better he was pleased. Besides he was a poor administrator.

Asafudaulah was 26 years old when his father Shujaudaulah died in 1775. He was the only heir of the late ruler and was most unprepared to rule. Asafudaulah did not care for the army. He was happy to cut down the security forces on the advice of the British so that he could use the same money on pleasures close to his heart. When his mother tried to warn Asafudaulah of the consequences, he fled Faizabad to rule from Lucknow. In Lucknow Asafudaulah went on a building binge that the city had never witnessed before. He is great because he transformed the city from a prosperous, but rustic marketplace into an urbane imperial capital.

The Mughal dynasty had reached the autumn of its glorious rule that began with Babur in the 16th century. The rulers of Avadh no longer felt subordinate to Delhi. Asafudaulah had the means and power to make his capital look more lavish than that city. In haughty competition, he built a 60-foot-tall portal just opposite Akbar Gate and called it the Rumi Gate, after Rome, but with ornamental designs stolen from Moorish architecture and in imitation of gates in Istanbul. Asafudaulah adored everything European, including Claude Martin, the soldier who had arrived here penniless from France. After the defeat of France by the British in India, many Frenchmen like Martin found themselves without a job. Some were imprisoned, others deported and a few befriended by local rulers against the British, a common enemy.

The first Frenchmen in Lucknow had settled down in the Firangi Mahal area. They had traded horses when Lucknow was still a little cluster of about 20 villages. Martin came to Lucknow later, perhaps with Asafudaulah, and soon earned the reputation of being an expert in much. The landlocked population watched him fly hot air balloons, make gunpowder explode and design the best buildings in town. He taught friends how to gamble and get rich instantly. Martin made most of his money in bets with the king and by defeating His Majesty in numerous cockfights.

SAHARA CITY

Munna Bhai drags a chair and sits down with us. We pretend not to hear the loud slurps every time the teacup touches his lips. He is obviously enjoying his tea. He says that helicopters are flying in VIP guests like Amitabh Bachchan to Sahara City for the weddings of two young men from the Sahara family. Hundreds of Mercedes Benz sedans hired to ferry some 10,000 guests from the airport to participate in the celebrations are the cause of the traffic jam. The joyous ceremony is expected to continue for an entire week. Even as we talk, Chinese acrobats along with ballet dancers from abroad prepare to entertain visitors, and the London Philharmonic Orchestra makes music in-between plaster of Paris pillars lit up with fire.

Munna Bhai says he was inside Sahara City a few hours ago, and saw it all. He shows us a photograph of himself shaking the hand of Shahrukh Khan, and another one with Aishwarya Rai, who drapes a slender arm around his waist.

Among numerous cooks invited from different parts of the country, Munna Bhai has been requested to serve his kebabs at the banquet, where Mexican food competes with the mouthwatering cuisine of Maharashtra. Thousands of homeless people have been promised free food during the week-long festivities, and Subrata Roy paid for the marriage of 101 couples from poor families before the wedding of the two brothers from the Sahara family was formalised.

"What are you waiting for? Take us with you. Show us what is going on." Bano Bua gets up to go, expecting Munna Bhai to follow her. But Munna Bhai looks down at his feet and finds a spot under the chair that he vigorously rubs with one foot.

"The security is tight, Bua. Everyone needs a microchip-embedded invitation that is scanned at the gate..." Munna Bhai is apologetic.

Bano Bua does not quite understand the real reason why we are unable to participate in the most lavish event held in Lucknow since the marriage of Billo Rani, the favourite cat of Wajid Ali Shah. Almost a century and a half ago, the British had rudely interrupted the wedding of Billo Rani before Wajid Ali Shah, the last ruler of Avadh, was forced out of his kingdom in 1856. At the wedding, His Majesty had found it difficult to keep his bejewelled fingers out of Billo Rani's silky Persian coat. But he avoided looking into her large, wide eyes that to his discomfort resembled an ocean flooded with questions. Once he noticed that Billo Rani was beginning to brood, he decided to get her married.

He sent for Aman and Aiman, the two sisters responsible for combing the city to find the most beautiful women for His Majesty's *parikhana,* the royal harem.

Once the two sisters had found the perfect match for Billo Rani, preparations for the cat wedding began months before the actual ceremony. The large community of professional jesters pulled out their costumes and split into groups to entertain people at every street corner. The European vocalist Mario was summoned to play the drums for the king, who wore a saffron robe to match the colour of the palace walls of Kaiserbagh. The crown was given a break and his curly locks were freed as His Majesty turned in endless circles like a mystic. The air was filled with anticipation of the first sound from the flute in playful memory of Lord Krishna, before an unrestricted number of people were allowed to walk in and out of the palace gates, wide open during the auspicious ceremony. As His Majesty danced, he also sang the lyrics composed by him for the occasion to the mournfully melodious tune of *Raga Bhairavi.*

> Oh, father, look! I am soon gone away from home,
> I see four bearers decorate the palanquin,
> That will take me away from those close,
> And those who are not.
> This porch is already like the faraway peak of a mountain,
> This courtyard is now land unknown.
> Oh, father! Keep this home to yourself then,
> I am now on my way with the groom,
> To another den.

Elsewhere in the city, *pahalwans* had wrestled within rings made by lovers of the sport and gamblers gathered to bet on fighter cocks on the slopes of the Gomti, which allowed fish to be caught by nets woven only in silver thread. Archers shot arrows between guards from the Banka, Tircha, Ghanghor, Akhtari or Nadri brigades, while lancers raced astride horses with tails and manes streaked orange with henna. And the rainbow laughed to see such sport from behind countless kites more colourful than itself.

The British barged in to spoil the fun and games. They gate-crashed into the gaiety and got His Majesty to pack his bags and leave Avadh.

After Bano Bua has finished crying over the departure of Wajid Ali Shah from his beloved Lucknow, she says she cannot understand why anyone would want to be imprisoned inside Sahara City, even if it is for a wedding.

"The wedding of the Sahara boys sounds like a celebration in jail. And who wants to go to prison, anyways," she concludes once she figures out that Munna Bhai is not influential enough to escort two uninvited guests with him to Sahara City. This is rarely done in a town famous to this day for its fathomless hospitality, poetically called *daryadili* in Urdu. In Lucknow people do not wait for an invite to join fellow citizens in joyous times and in moments of tragedy.

"How times are changing," mutters Bano Bua as she makes herself a little more comfortable at the Kebab Korner and continues to speak to Munna Bhai about other matters. Soon both of them step out to continue talking outside the kiosk.

TROUBLE ON THE STREET

When Bano Bua returns, she is sweating.

"There is a big problem, Bibi," she says.

"Bua, please tell me what the problem is."

"The Zaidi community that lives across the river has decided to recite *nohas* and dirge, to perform *matam* on the street this year, all the way to Karbala on the other side of the city. This has never been done before. For hundreds of years Muharram has been observed in the old city. Even those Muslims living in newer neighbourhoods like ourselves go to old Lucknow to perform prayers or worship privately at home."

Karbala at Talkatora in the south-west of the city is the place for pilgrims during Muharram. About 200 years ago, an Indian pilgrim was caught in a sectarian quarrel in the original Karbala in southern Iraq. He returned home safely to Lucknow with a metal crest that had crowned the staff of Abbas, a brave stepbrother of Husain who was also killed on the 10th of Muharram in Karbala in 680.

Each year at Muharram, processions from around the city congregate at the local Karbala to touch their banner with the relic of Abbas, kept in a sacred monument erected by one of the most devout Shia rulers of Lucknow. At that time, a military guard holding banners had sauntered behind a column of elephants carrying mourners, followed by a mourner-in-chief and then the king and his male companions.

An Arab steed dressed in saddlecloth woven in gold and silver carried on its back a turban, a bow and some arrows, with its hooves dyed in red in memory of the blood shed by the martyred Husain and his wounded steed. The horse in the procession was flanked by costumed attendants. The queen's procession with matching paraphernalia that included cooks, storytellers, tailors and hairdressers trailed behind, ahead of a crowd of a hundred others, some reciting verses from the Koran.

The mourners congregated at Karbala at the grand replica of the tomb of Husain for the last rites.

"It will be alright, Bua." I feel my voice quiver. "It seems like this is a small group of people that does not mean anyone any harm. And if they want to pass through here, why not let them?" I console Bano Bua, craning my neck over the crowd, trying to get a glimpse of the procession of Shias, whose sorrowful song and rhythmic beats had crawled closer.

"What are you saying? That is not the only problem."

"What then is the other problem?"

"Bibi, there is a Hindu marriage procession on its way from the opposite direction, on the same path. Can you imagine what will happen once the two groups collide? Think of two trains rolling towards each other on the same track—bang!" Bano Bua slaps her hands together.

"People have been talking to both communities for days, I am told. But neither the Hindu merrymakers nor the Muslim mourners are willing to listen to anyone. Both insist that they have instructions from the divine to perform their respective rituals at the same appointed hour and not a minute before or after."

"Now the crowd waits, wondering what to expect next," Bano Bua continues, all her talk drowning in a thunderous fusion of the measured drumming.

This is a painful moment for those who are proud to be the offspring of the Ganga and Yamuna way of life. The people have been spoon-fed over centuries on customs as contradictory as the course followed by the two rivers that nevertheless converge happily in Allahabad, at the holy site of sangam. This is not too far from Lucknow, and "Ganga-Jamuni" is always uttered in a single breath in Lucknow in lyrical support of the symbiotic confluence of all that is noble in both the Hindu and Muslim views of the world.

> I become you.
> You become me.
> I am the soul
> You are the heart.
> How can they claim,
> I am apart.
> You are apart?

Amir Khusro sings about his relationship with the creator of the world, but Khusro is great precisely because the same lines also pay tribute to the glorious Gangetic plains where he was born and feels so at home.

I go running out of the Kebab Korner to stand on the rim of quite a spectacle. The listless crowd awaits action. I feel Bano Bua's fingers locked into my own.

I hear Munna Bhai shout instructions. I see Naresh appear out of nowhere, hurrying towards us, carrying on his shoulder a long, wooden ladder. Teenaged boys run back and forth on the pavement in excitement. A group of not more than five women, holding the hands of several small children, two of them carrying infants in the arms, are moved away from under a street lamp and flock closer to the kiosk.

Some energetic limbs help Naresh to balance the ladder, made out of bamboo.

Munna Bhai hurries up to where Bano Bua stands hugging my arm. He looks at Bano Bua and then at me and shakes his head as if he wishes we had not been there. His eyes mirror memories of the millions of people already hated and hacked by men claiming to love God more than human beings.

Thoughts of a bloodbath make Naresh panic and he dares to hurry and push Bano Bua towards the ladder, making her slip and slide. She drags me with her.

Naresh continues to force a silent, subdued Bano Bua to climb up the ladder onto the terrace, where several arms already dangle down to take her hand. I follow, scrambling to a safe landing on my hands and legs.

The other women and children come to the terrace after me. The infants are given back to the women by other helping hands behind them. Rising above the group of women, children and some elderly men, unknown to me, who squat on the floor of the rooftop, I tip myself taller on the toes. When I stretch over to one side I see a scene that resembles a shot out of the popular film *Monsoon Wedding*. People dressed in glittering accessories and bright clothes jerk their bodies forward to funky beats of party-time tunes from the same film. In the middle of musicians and dancers, a majestic horse trots, decked in equally dazzling drapes and shimmering streamers. The animal is led by a short figure sporting a big turban. It marshals on closer to the front line of mourners on one side of the street, with the happy people hopping, skipping and jumping beside it.

The one astride the horse has to be the groom. He is decorated in marriage finery, his face made invisible by a thick curtain strung together with flowers. He is on his way to meet the bride, waiting probably across the bridge.

I don't know which side to look. I turn right and left, able to enjoy both the pageant of gloom here and that of glad tidings there. I hear the soundtrack of modern cinema mingle with sombre songs about the past. I smile at one without feeling the need to frown at the other.

Waves of hurt waft into lyrics of love; the clang of cymbals chorus with beats on human breasts. There is no need for the vision to pendulate anymore. The two caravans in front of me are sharing the same space. The mission of the two is totally opposite to the other. Both refuse to pause at the crossroad in confrontation. Instead, I see them sail past each other like two ships, even providing a patch to the other. I am able to breathe again. The crowd has dispersed to make way for a platoon of policemen speeding upon the scene, once again in chase of problems that do not exist. The citizens have already resolved the problem, if there was any, on their own and with grace.

"Lucknow is different. This can only happen in Lucknow," I whisper to myself as I allow the 1945 composition of Majaz soothe the soul.

> Paradise of beauty, love lane of grace,
> Is Lucknow.
> Flowers bloom,
> In every eye like a poem.
> Trees of tolerance,
> Refuge of Turks,
> Home to many races,
> Is Lucknow.
> Maidens here,
> The envy of every Cleopatra there.
> Each corner a crowd of colour,
> Picturesque paths,
> Buds a playful poet.
> The parlour of Shiraz,
> Is Lucknow,
> Here songsters sprout.
> There is wine,
> And clouds promise showers.
> Swords unsheathe to thundering clap,
> Virgins unveil hidden darts.
> The soul of Lucknow,
> The seed of elegance,
> Bewitches Spring till eternity.
> Poppy the obsession though,
> Musk the madness,
> In the garden,
> That is Lucknow.
> Awkward tear,
> Soils the wear,
> Of the short visit,
> Of the wanderer.
> Sprinkle not the flowerbed with disrepute.
> Before the air is spoiled,

By the heir of Yusuf,
Allow dawn,
To water a new way.
May the evening full of ruin,
Remain a memory,
Even after Majaz has called it a day.

I am happy to have experienced the city in its best mood. I am hopeful. We celebrate life in Lucknow by weeping in each other's arms. Then the wooden ladder gives way to the monkeying of many.

Naresh lies plastered to the ground on his back beside broken pieces of the ladder. The tray that he had been bringing to the rooftop has landed on his face. All the snacks that had flown out of his hand have been caught by street urchins, who have managed to dodge the spill of hot tea.

Munna Bhai performs a multiple-paced double jig and Naresh joins the prancing without bother for fractures to his bones. Others come, moving in step to music that plays only in their mind. For the sound of both the marriage and mourners has already receded far, far away.

Bano Bua and I, the last two refugees left on the terrace, wait to be brought down by another ladder. The crowd is already beginning to thin, allowing the breeze to finally fan its way towards us. Chairs and tables are dragged out of the kiosk in a commotion and arranged in a circle on the pavement.

"This is Chandan," says a sweating Munna Bhai, who seems to want more song and dance.

But Bano Bua reminds us that we are in the midst of mourning and Muharram. We should celebrate less and reflect more during this month than at any other time of the year.

We should ponder the meaning of birth and death and what we wish to make of our lives on Earth. This is also one occasion to sieve out what is important in life from what is not.

And after having said all this, Bano Bua sits down as if in wait for us to lower ourselves to the floor to touch her feet in respect, in obedience and in adoration.

SHAH NAJAF

"Oh, Munna, my heart flutters. It feels like a butterfly lost in a bush. It has been years since I meditated during Muharram. Powers beyond my knowledge beckon me to offer my prayers. Is it possible at all for you to take me to pray at the Shah Najaf?"

Bano Bua is forlorn surely because we did not bow before her, but continued to stand firm where we stood at considerable distance from where she had chosen to rest. And she continues to moan and groan and fish for attention.

"Bano Bua, I will take you there. And anywhere else that you might want to go. I have my car parked at the end of the street," Chandan interrupts.

"Where is the tea, boys? What is taking you so long to bring two cups of tea?" Munna Bhai's loud command sails towards the kitchen. "Have tea and then Chandan Bhai will take you to the Shah Najaf," he says, turning back to us.

"May God bless you for your kind offer, but I don't think I know you, son..." Bano Bua looks closer at Chandan, leaning towards him across the table on an elbow.

"Chandan Bhai is the hero of the hour. He has not slept for three nights, Bua. He was talking to the Hindu family...then to the Muslim family. He had patiently listened to both. He was constantly going back and forth, trying to make sure that nobody did anything that should not be done, that might bring sorrow and shame upon us all." Munna Bhai hugs Chandan.

Chandan comes from the Hindu family that more than a hundred years ago built a shrine to Husain after an ancestor prayed to the grandson of Muhammad and was blessed with a son. The shrine remains open to the public during Muharram and throughout the year. Chandan prays there all the time. He says that he has learnt from his elders to live in comfort with all the different ways of life of his neighbours, also making sure that he gets the respect he deserves in return from them.

From his ancestors, Chandan has inherited an unshakeable belief in the essential goodness of Husain, making it natural for him to practice the rituals at Muharram even as he remains a Hindu.

"Where would you like to go first? To the Shah Najaf, or should I drive you home?" Chandan wants to know.

"It is four o'clock in the morning, son. Let me enjoy the lark, a little longer. I would like to say my morning prayers at the Shah Najaf before returning home." Bano Bua stands up.

"Naresh, please return home and remember that there is no time to sleep anymore. Sweep the porch and make sure that there is water stored in the kitchen and in the bathrooms.

"Don't just sit there staring at me...Come here and take the house keys, you lazy bag of bones." Bano Bua walks towards Naresh, who shoots up on his feet, having stolen a little pause on the haunches. He takes the keys from Bano Bua and disappears as fast as he can.

We walk away from the kiosk along with Chandan and Munna Bhai towards another dawn.Wreaths of tiny electric lights worn around the majestic rooftop of the Carlton Hotel blink as we drive past the property, part of which has been converted into a shopping mall.

Chandan parks the car a little away from the low, whitewashed walls of the Shah Najaf. At this time of the year, all luxury is discouraged, including driving in comfort in a car. We leave our footwear inside the car and walk barefoot, in silence with the head covered, to join other pilgrims crowding the Shah Najaf premises. People walk in and out of the imposing gateway; they crowd the paved courtyard and the marble steps that lead into the mausoleum, built in the early 19th century in imitation of the tomb of Ali in Iraq.

We walk into the central chamber that is lit up with a thousand candles and whatever else is left of the chandelier that was once strung with precious stones. The light is blinding as it bounces back from many mirrors stained by time, their golden frames still decorating the walls.

There is no room for Chandan and Munna Bhai in this corner where I have followed Bano Bua. Here many women are already prostrate in prayer. Some sway in rhythm to the recitation of holy words close to their hearts. I find a place to my left and sit down on the floor, and Bano Bua disappears behind a canopy to perform the ablution customary before each prayer. She returns to face the direction of Mecca, home of the holy Kaaba in the Arabian Peninsula, while I wonder about the many wives of the ruler.

My vision traces the burial place of King Ghaziuddin Haidar Shah in the main hall and the eyes squint at the amount of silver decoration on the tomb. To the right side of the royal grave my gaze rests on the remains of Mubarak Mahal, an English beauty. Her charm and literary talents had instantly stolen the heart of His Majesty. This was during a visit to the neighbouring city of Kanpur where Ghaziuddin Haidar met Warren Hastings, British India's Governor General, in 1818.

Ghaziuddin's ancestors had governed Lucknow on behalf of Delhi since 1720, but lost the Battle of Buxar in 1764 to the British. Almost a century later Delhi's majestic fortunes had finally ebbed, and Hastings persuaded Avadh to declare autonomy from Delhi in 1819. After the Kanpur summit with Hastings, Ghaziuddin exchanged his title of a mere naib, or representative in Avadh of Delhi, to independent ruler. (The title nawab is just the anglicised pronunciation of naib.) He was the first king of Avadh. Ghaziuddin was convinced by the British to give up much territory but made sure that he was allowed to keep Lucknow as his capital, more impressive than Delhi.

Nasiruddin Haider, Muhammad Ali, Amjad Ali Shah and Wajid Ali Shah succeeded Ghaziuddin, and the last ruler was forced to abdicate in 1856. This was followed by the 1857 uprising that went down in history as South Asia's first war of independence from the British.

Along with a crown, Ghaziuddin also won the hand of 16-year-old Mariam, the European maiden who taught English to her husband. The couple had enjoyed boating and riding together. Mariam always appeared unveiled in public, and was responsible for adding a certain European flavour to Lucknow and earning for the city its second title of the Paris of the East.

Vilayati Bagh was a sprawling garden where Mubarak Begum enjoyed English-style tea parties with her middle-aged husband, who loved listening to western music playing at an impressive bandstand built in the centre of the garden.

Sarfaraz Mahal, the Sunni Muslim wife of the king, is buried next to Ghaziuddin and Mubarak Mahal. Under the same roof rests Mumtaz Mahal, a Hindu wife whose love for bangles had made minions dash harum-scarum to find the most exquisite in the kingdom. Mumtaz Mahal liked to run bangles from her forearm down to her wrists, mainly to conceal the many tattoos that may have reminded her of her not-so-regal background. She built a mosque before her death that still stands in the city, but it is in ruins. Will someone restore the vanished glory of the common heritage of all citizens of Lucknow or allow yet another heritage property to vanish away from memory?

By the time Bano Bua finished praying, the morning sun had exchanged its marigold smile for a frown, as if from a furnace. It is not yet midday but it is already very warm.

I am thirsty. I can hardly wait to wash away all the grit that has gathered on my skin over the last couple of hours.

I give my face a gentle scrub, and looking around notice that most of the pilgrims are at last at peace after their night-long vigil. Bodies are strewn all over the sacred premise in deep sleep, and some snore while sitting. Munna Bhai is there as well, walking towards us from the opposite direction, a handkerchief knotted around his head like a skullcap.

Before Munna Bhai can offer us refreshments at his stall once again, I suggest that we go home.

TAMBOLI BEGUM

So Chandan drives us to our doorstep.

Naresh lets us in and goes back to taking care of early morning chores. In the absence of Bano Bua, he has got the radio running in one corner of the kitchen counter. As he cleans crockery and cutlery, he hums along to an Asha Bhosle song playing on the radio.

> Do I hear someone call me,
> Is someone also sad?
> Restless with longing for me?
> What place is this,
> Friends?
> What abode is it?

Bano Bua is about to scold Naresh for using the radio without her permission. Instead she freezes in the doorway. Once she had reached home, Naresh had promptly switched the radio off and stopped singing. Unbelievable, but true. Bano Bua is asking Naresh to play the radio and also to increase the volume. She also tells him that there is no need for him to sing along. She looks excited as she listens to the end of the same song.

She turns around and tells me that she knows what the Baba of the Bottles means. She says that she has the answer to the riddle of the Baba. The song playing on the radio is from Bollywood. This is the song of the courtesan who is singing on the return to her place of birth, from where she had been kidnapped nearly two decades ago. On screen she tries to recognise her home, wondering if her parents and brother still remember her. In-between the singing, the mother appears on screen. Having sensed her daughter's presence, the mother wonders if her little girl has come home.

The character of the mother is played by Tamboli Begum. The daughter is played by the actress who in another film is shown singing and romancing in the midst of one of Holland's endless tulip fields.

> The eternal lament of your look
> Seeing flowers as a wall
> Between us.
> When dreams have led to more
> Visible as far as the eye can see
> Is a life full of blossoms galore.

And petal by petal, Bano Bua tries to unravel the relationship between Tulip Blossom and Tamboli Begum. *Tamboli* is the upside-down way that people here pronounce Istanbul, just like they have played around with other words, like changing the name of their own city Lucknow to *nakhlau*. The obelisk of Colonel John Collins, a British resident of Lucknow in the early 19th century, is better known as *kallan ki laat*, while

Queen Victoria Street is shortened to *turia* by the rather innovative *nakhlauwalas.*

As mentioned earlier, "begum" refers to a woman of high rank. Bano Bua suspects that the Baba of the Bottles' Tulip Blossom is none other than our very own Tamboli Begum. What all the four words of tulip, blossom, *tamboli* and begum have in common is a Turkic ancestry. Tamboli Begum's Turkic ancestors from Central Asia crossed into Europe, and later came to Avadh through Persia many generations ago. The tulip flower grows in the mountains of Central Asia and it travelled westwards, perhaps in the pockets of horsemen galloping towards newfound lands in the plains. Because it looks like a headdress, the flower gets its name from *tulband,* the Farsi word for turban. There is a mention of tulips in the *Memoirs of Babur,* whose author brought the flower from Afghanistan to India in the early 16th century.

Bano Bua is happy with her conclusions and with the way she thinks she has connected all the dots. She gives five minutes to Naresh to get ready and to take her to the residence of Tamboli Begum.

"Bibi, do you get it or not? It is Tamboli Begum who knows why your groom is taking so long to come to your doorstep. Her reputation as an actress pales compared to her prowess as a fortune teller and miracle maker. She makes things happen, you know. We must see her as soon as possible," Bano Bua insists.

Bano Bua has got me excited at the thought of meeting Tamboli Begum, one of the senior-most citizens of the city and an endless enigma. She is a psychic in spirit and player on screen. The different winds from different directions that blow across Lucknow never tire of sharing lots of stories about the virtues of Tamboli Begum.

I do not want to see Tamboli Begum because I want her to help me get a groom. I am curious to find out what her fatwa-waving fingers look like.

I suggest to Bano Bua that we should wait for the first caravan of stars to quickly twinkle across the deepening blue sky before stepping out of the house. But Bano Bua wants to go *now* in the sunshine. So I tell her to go with Naresh to Tamboli Begum by herself.

Which she does, returning home many hours later, only after the *saptarshi* is visible in the sky and the first rainfall of the season has washed away the discomfort suffered collectively by a city during the intense heat of the summer months.

These are some of the stories that she brought back for me about tulips and elephants from the long-overdue visit to Tamboli Begum.

Bano Bua is given the address of Tamboli Begum by Miss Madhavi, who knows Tamboli Begum well and even requested her to give Bano Bua an audience.

Bano Bua arrives at Tamboli Begum's sprawling ancestral home, called Tamboli Tola. She lives by herself and has one large bedroom. The rest of the rooms (over a dozen) are shared with other women, together with whom she is trying to make a difference in the world. She is single and successful. She is single because she never wanted to marry anyone—or perhaps the truth is quite the opposite. She is successful because she has always been the lord and master of her life. She allows her head and heart to fulfil every potential, without focus on one talent at the expense of another, and she hardly ever withholds a desire.

Bano Bua enters Tamboli Tola and pauses in the courtyard to witness women of different age groups dressed in saris or draped in dyed cotton dupattas, talking, laughing and engrossed in different activities in different parts of this home. In one corner a group of women pound herbs into powder. Another group of women package the powdered spices into bags that come in various colours and sizes. Bano Bua has never seen such a happy group of so many women, except in a painting by a Lucknow College of Arts and Crafts artist; it has been hanging forever on one of the walls in our home.

She looks elsewhere and notices one more woman standing on the threshold of the verandah in front. When she catches Bano Bua's eye, she smiles and greets her with an *adaab.* Bano Bua is welcomed and asked to follow her through an inner courtyard, also abuzz with other activities like fine hand embroidery on chiffons and on muslin cloths. There are many more clusters of women who are busy knitting, while others merrily work on sewing machines.

As her polite escort stops to knock on a large wooden door, Bano Bua quickly peeps into the adjoining rooms, filled with children reciting poems and learning to read and write, not just *alif, bey, pe* but also a, b, c.

When the door in front of her finally opens, the already overawed Bano Bua finds herself staring at a smiling Tamboli Begum. Such *rubaru* proximity with Tamboli Begum makes Bano Bua nervous. But Tamboli Begum is used to the effect that her presence has on people, especially those who meet her for the first time; she steps forth to make friends.

"There are many men in this household as well. But they are busy in the kitchen. They tend to the garden, or you can spy them plumbing or repairing the electricity," says Tamboli Begum, and after making that important announcement, she invites Bano Bua into her inner chamber.

The outer room is decorated with shelves holding lamps in the shape of the tulip flower. A many-hued chandelier in a similar shape hangs down the middle of the ceiling.

Watching Bano Bua admire the ware placed on several racks, Tamboli Begum laughs loudly.

Bano Bua looks at her in embarrassment.

"The world thinks that tulips are from Holland. The Dutch earn a lot of money from selling tulip bulbs today. But when the first shipload of the bulbs landed in Antwerp in the 16th century from Turkey, the Dutch tried to eat them!"

Tamboli Begum continues to laugh and to talk. She says that the Dutch had coated the tulip bulb with sugar and bitten into it again and again, but their greed had gotten them nowhere. This is followed by more laughter, which is so infectious that Bano Bua bursts into roaring mirth as well.

Tulips grow wild in the Central Asian mountain range of the Pamir. The flower became a favourite in Europe in the 17th century after it was painted by Flemish artist Jan Brueghel the Elder. A Dutch botanist was the first to cultivate tulips in his garden, arousing the interest of other horticulturalists in the flower. Soon thousands of varieties of tulips were cultivated and sold for a price. Around 1633, the flower became so precious that it was used for barter, and for a basket of tulip bulbs it was possible to get a house. The flower had followed the path of Turkic warriors employed by Persian rulers, who conquered European and Persian lands to make a home far away from Central Asia, in modern-day Turkey.

"You think the rulers of Avadh were decadent? That is because you don't know the eccentricities of some of the medieval rulers of Istanbul. One was so impossibly *lattoo* over the tulip that he engaged the entire energy of the nation into creating everything around him to look like a tulip. He listened to no one and a time came when courtiers decided to dethrone and murder the ruler for having drained the national treasury to fulfil his whims."

The young woman who had brought Bano Bua to Tamboli Begum had quietly left.

"Do not believe what is whispered about me in the city and what is written about me in newspapers and magazines," Tamboli Begum advises Bano Bua, offering her to sit on a chair that faces her own.

"The media does not have the patience to find out who I really am. Reporters come to me when they hear that I have worked in a film with a famous actor or director. The questions they ask me are about the celebrities I know. They are not interested in me. They are interested only in celebrities who are out of reach for them. The media says that I am a witch, a magician, and I enjoy supernatural powers. What rubbish! All of it is untrue. I am nothing, but at the same time I am everything.

"Now you tell me what makes you believe that I can find a groom for your girl. If she wants a groom, she will find one. And if she is unable to do so, so what? Your job is not to make the one you love feel inadequate in life just because she is not able to fulfil *your* dream. Please let her be. Your only job in life is to take care of yourself and then attend to whoever is with you at that particular point in time. What you don't have in life is not worth the fret.

"Now have you had enough? Do you want to leave, or do you want to know who I really am and where I come from?" questions Tamboli Begum, her henna-red hair shimmering in the afternoon light and her cheekbones glowing.

Bano Bua cannot take her eyes away from Tamboli Begum and wants her to go on talking.

"My complexion is pale but my ancestors were dark-skinned. In fact, very dark-skinned. My *nana* resembled a Nubian because, hundreds of years ago, a harassed Nubian somewhere in the northern part of Africa jumped into the river Nile to swim away from all his troubles on land. In his favour was his youth and a talisman in the shape of an elephant given to him by his grandmother. This he had clutched tight in one fist through the high tide and man-swallowing whirlpools. In fact, the talisman had helped the fleeing Nubian to overcome deadly rocks and life-threatening rapids. He was able to ride on the backs of killer crocodiles and use the Egyptian cobras to pull him upstream till he was dropped by the Nile into the more friendly flow of the Mediterranean Sea.

The sun, sand and wind of his wondrous new surroundings had revived his breath. Life on the coast of this sea was fruitful for the Nubian and his generation increased in number. Although no longer just Nubian, his descendants of various complexions filled the earth. Some went on to rule over the fish in the sea and others mastered the birds in the sky. A few centuries later one of his descendants was seen flaunting a chain with a silver cross around his neck, which was no longer as dark as ebony. But in all these centuries, the elephant talisman has never left the body of any Nubian.

When medieval inquisitions in the name of heaven made life hell for human beings in Europe, my ancestor, the Nubian, took refuge somewhere, from where he was sadly kidnapped and taught how to be a successful pirate. When he tired of living only on the sea, he escaped to a life on land and befriended a trader heading eastwards to Istanbul. They turned their backs on the dark continent in search of light. On the way, the two shared such great stories that they fell in love. The sheer power of their love for each other led them through an adventurous journey filled with ecstasies and agonies into fields upon fields of tulips. Here, cradled in one of the deepest red blossoms, a *bano* was born to them. One day this African, European, Semitic and Turkic *bano* bumped into a nawab from Lucknow on one of the prettiest streets of Istanbul's Sultanahmet Square. It was love at first sight and a wedding soon followed.

When the couple returned to Lucknow, the groom's mother wanted to know if the *bano* was a Shia Muslim or not. The answer was little more than a shrug that made the mother-in-law furious—but she still organised festivities that lasted an entire month in the hope of a grandson. Instead, Tamboli Begum was born to the newlyweds in Lucknow, sometime in the middle of the last century.

"See that one there," Tamboli Begum points to a tiny artefact in one corner of the cupboard.

"Yes, Tamboli Begum, I do see it. Do you mean that Ganesha there?" replies Bano Bua.

"Ganesha to you, but also Kush the Nubian to me," smiles Tamboli Begum, allowing Bano Bua to take leave after having enjoyed several cups of tea and some samosas.

As Bano Bua prepares to go, Tamboli Begum asks one of her girls to gift her a bag.

"Take this bag of samosas and share them with all the arrogant people around you. Tell them that the potatoes that make the filling of a samosa so mouthwatering have come from southern Peru and faraway Bolivia. Tell them who say the potato is theirs and garlic is ours that most of the ingredients in a samosa are from outside the region of South Asia. Those who say that saffron is theirs and green is ours, that India is theirs and Pakistan is ours, must know that the original cultivation of onions is claimed by several civilisations including China, Egypt and Iran. Chillies are from Mexico, garlic from central Asia, China and Siberia. While South Asia introduced ginger and south India taught the world to use turmeric, coriander was once the main ingredient in Greek medicines. The yummy crust of the samosa is made from wheat. Humans first made a delicious meal of the grain around the Mediterranean coast. Salt is from different parts of the earth and is responsible for the rise and fall of empires worldwide. The art of deep-frying food is a skill learnt from the Egyptians.

"Ask all those who believe in the clash, and not in the continuity of cultures, if they are aware that there would be no samosa without the *samsa,* a popular snack all over Central Asia. Except that the *samsa* is a refined wheat flour preparation and is stuffed with minced mutton. I had ordered a *samsa* once on a street in Tashkent, in modern-day Uzbekistan. As I waited for this ancestor of my beloved samosa to bake in a clay oven, I thought that there would be no samosa without a *samsa,* just like there would be no you without me and no me without you."

Tears roll down Tamboli Begum's face. She finds it difficult to go on talking. In a stern voice that quivers, she requests Bano Bua to go home. Tamboli Begum wants Bano Bua to hurry back, before the next cloudburst on the first day of the monsoon season makes it difficult for her to commute through the slushy, muddy and potholed roads of present-day Lucknow.

ACKNOWLEDGEMENTS

I take this opportunity to express heartfelt gratitude to Kumi Chandra, Anil Chandra and Kakul Hai for taking time to read the manuscript even before it was finished and for assuring me that I should continue to work on it.

I greatly appreciate the patience of Saachi Khurana, my editor at Niyogi Books, for having carefully ironed out convoluted emotions and vocabulary from the manuscript. Thank you, Shraboni Roy, for the very nice cover design in grey. That is the zone in which we try to live life in the city, trying to avoid extremities of both black and white. Above all, I remain indebted to the colourful citizens of Lucknow who continue to floor me with the kind of love and affection they practice at a time when hate is being forced upon us.

Lucknow may be economically and politically bankrupt today, but what is not in short supply here is lots of love among human beings. This is dedicated to that special way that love and life still exist in Lucknow.